The Fall of Albion Bay

ISBN: 979-8-8480-4643-4

Published by Paul Butler

THE FALL OF ALBION BAY

A MODERN SATIRE

PAUL BUTLER

*Paul is from the East End of
London and writes satire and literary fiction.*

To frontline people everywhere battling to perform their daily duties despite the obstacles created by the inept above them.

MONDAY

A new life was meant to start for Arnie Smeggins that morning, and in a strange way it did. He was about to become the most famous janitor in the world.

The early sunshine was already flooding his bedroom when the alarm sprang him to life. He peered at the time and blinked, he hadn't seen this silly hour in a while. The sun sure wakes up early in May. With a bounce Arnie flew out of bed, washed and shaved, and was out of the apartment before he knew it.

He at last had a job again.

At the bus stop his nerves jangled. Finally the months of searching were over, the despair and rejections behind him. The feelings of worthlessness when Lucy had called him a *forty-something potbellied lump on the scrapheap* as she had stormed out that night were now a thing of the past. He was starting to get over her, and what's more he was on his way to work. He had never given up, never shirked from the thankless grind of job hunting, and now at long last he was somebody again.

And as he stood at that bus stop a strange sensation slowly came over him. He finally recognised himself once more.

Half an hour later Arnie Smeggins stood and gazed at the impressive nine storey block before him. The headquarters of the famous Greater Albion Bay Company with mineral extraction sites all over the world. A grand cream coloured art deco front loomed above him, where on either side of a central façade hung two huge anchor emblems, each with '*Since 1855*' inscribed around them. This place oozed success and permanence; if he couldn't make this job stick his life may just as well be over.

Arnie bounded up the external steps and through some revolving doors, where a concierge cocked his head to glance at the letter in Arnie's hand.

"Ah yes sir, this is the staff entrance alright," the smartly uniformed man in his fifties said, as without fuss he answered an intercom and at the same time helped a woman who had forgotten her staff card through the turnstile. By his polite and efficient bearing this guy with the clipped tone was probably ex-military. Arnie looked down at immaculate pressed trousers; a pair of gleaming shoes shone back up.

Yep, that seals it, definitely ex-forces.

"And your name again sir?"

"Mr Smeggins, Arnold Smeggins, I'm to report to a Mr Slade. I'm the new janitor here."

"Ah welcome to the brigade Mr Smeggins, you'll find Mr Slade on Floor 8. Lift is straight across the lobby there."

"Thanks," said Arnie as he pushed his thigh through the barrier.

"And if you're gonna be working here you'd better get used to calling me Roger every morning."

"Sure Roger, will do."

"And a heads up," the man leaned in with a downward slant to his head, as if whispering outside the barracks about a surprise officer inspection at dawn. "There's a new Chief Exec starting today too, a Mr Devoux, so best look sharp lad, eyes front. Especially if they give you one of the top floors to look after. Your work will be on parade, in full view of the top brass as it were."

"Oh ok, thanks I'll be on my toes. And Mr. Slade is on Floor 8 you say?"

"Aye, and welcome to Albion, Mr Smeggins."

Arnie wasn't sure if Roger had saluted, but it sure felt like it.

He crossed the busy lobby and glanced back, if those other four concierges working the entrance barriers were half as on the ball as him this place sure was secure. And nice of Roger to give him the heads up like that.

At Floor 8 the opening lift doors immediately revealed a sign announcing, *'Building Services, Manager J. Slade'*. Shit, he hadn't expected Slade to be right opposite the lift. He was just straightening his shirt in the lobby when the door burst open.

"Ah Arnie, good to see you, punctual too," a tall lean man in his fifties with an open necked shirt and rolled up sleeves bowled out with extended hand. "Great, we like that, punctuality is good, shows respect for the team. You've started well. Right then here's the rules. First rule, it's never James. I hate James. It's Jim. Got that, good."

"Er, yeah sure..."

"That is except when top brass are about, then it's Mr Slade."

"Sure J..."

"We're one big happy family here. Hardly any

3

complaints, no trouble, and few people leave. I've been here 25 years, started at the bottom, and my father was here before me. So work hard, be fair, and you'll love it. Got that, good."

"Yeah sure Jim got all that. So where do I start?"

"That's the spirit! Right get your arse down to basement, collect your trolley and overalls from Ron in Supplies, then get that same arse straight back here ready to get cracking. Got that, good."

Arnie reached the lift, but Slade was not done.

"And Arnie..."

"Huh?"

"Any problems, any balls ups, you tell me, or tell some-one, and we work together to sort it out. Then that's the end of it. My door is always open. But don't take any liberties, we don't put up with that, this is a top firm. No time for shirkers, moaners, or timewasters. Loyalty deserves loyalty. Got that, good."

Arnie nodded, yep that sounded straightforward enough.

But the basement that appeared a few moments later as the lift doors slid open did not look so straightforward. Ahead stretched a labyrinth of corridors with exposed pipes running along the ceiling, a constant hum of plant machinery, and detergent smells he had never known before.

Arnie began to step out as a sharp-suited little guy with a bright yellow tie barged into him. Arnie swerved, curved his body, and lifted his arm to let the rude little man duck safely under his armpit and into the lift.

Once out into the labyrinth Arnie sniffed the air, best just follow the smells of detergent. Eventually after marching up a few corridors, he saw that his hunch had been right. Emerging into an open space he gazed up at a large sign hanging from two chains which read *'Supplies.'*

His eyes widened. My, what a place!

Lined against the walls were countless stacked boxes, each labelled for dispatch to different company sites around the world. Further up, several corridors span away like the spokes of a wheel, each with beavering figures loading up containers and whatever else.

Everything seemed to be operating like clockwork.

Against one wall Arnie spotted a few trollies laden with cleaning equipment, each tagged with a handwritten instruction. One caught his eye. *'For Arnold Smeggins, 15th May. Collect mop and bucket from Supervisor.'*

Arnie looked around, across the way there was a split door that had its lower half closed. Behind the open top half was a brown overall with a supervisor in it. A look of serious contemplation clouded the man's face, as between strokes of his moustache he perused the tablet he was holding.

Arnie approached, "Ahem..."

No response.

"Excuse me."

Arnie straightened a little to peer over the top of the man's tablet. It said, *'Ron's Monthly Soap Order'.*

"What do you want?" mumbled the overall still looking at the tablet.

"It says over there that I need a mop and bucket."

"A bucket?"

"New janitor. I'm Smeggins, Mr Slade told me to come down here."

"How big?"

"Pardon?"

"How big do you want your bucket?"

"Normal I guess."

"Not done this before have you."

"No why?"

"Big decision picking your bucket."

"How so?"

"It's like a golfer's clubs. Too big for you it clanks about. Too small and you have to keep changing the water."

"Er well, medium will do."

"Oval or round?"

"Er oval."

"Silver or black?"

"Black. Can I have two mops?"

"We're out of black."

"OK. Silver then."

There was a rapid clatter as the brown overall lifted a bucket and mop over the half door and passed them across.

"Right then, here you are duly despatched, one silver oval bucket with castors pre-fitted for the purposes thereof, plus one mop duly supplied forthwith. Now sign here."

"I wanted two mops."

"Two mops!"

"I'm keen."

"Listen mate, it's one mop per day or I'll be cleaned out!"

"But..."

"Come back tomorrow if you want another mop. And when you get back to Slade give him your bucket assessment."

"Bucket assessment?"

"Peer review."

"What?"

"You know, tell us what you think of your bucket; very satisfied, satisfied, don't know... that sort of thing. That's how we improve, collecting feedback. Modern methods it is."

"Oh right."

"ARFA. Action Review Feedback Assessment. How can bucket quality improve if people using them don't give frontline feedback? Ask Slade for an ARFA form to assess the bucket, and don't forget to get him to countersign it. And take this key. Cleaning materials are in locked cupboards on each floor near the lifts. My staff refill them every morning. Your overalls are on the trolley, come back tomorrow and we'll have a spare set for you."

"So will I get a spare mop then as well?"

Ron sniffed with a slight twitch of the moustache, but the full attention of the brown overall had now firmly returned to the monthly soap order or whatever it was. Whoever the supplier was on the other end of that order had no chance.

* * *

Arnie threw his newly acquired mop and bucket onto his trolley and leaned in to get the thing moving. At the lift he checked nobody was about and pulled on his new blue overalls. They fitted perfectly. He patted the Albion crest on his chest, what a feeling! Now that he was fully dressed he was really part of something again.

If only Lucy could see him now! He would text her later about this.

Back up on eighth the lift doors slid open, and Arnie proudly wheeled his trolley into the lobby with the mop handle sticking out the front.

Slade did a double take. "Bloody 'ell! With that thing sticking out the front you look like Rommel!"

"*Who?*"

"Oh never mind."

"I've been evaluating my bucket in the lift...."

"Right now, to work Arnie..."

"Hey Jim," said a voice from the floor with a strong cockney accent. It was coming from a short blond guy with a mullet haircut who was pulling on a wrench under a radiator.

Slade grinned. "You still here Bob? I thought you were on nights. Has the missus thrown you out again?"

"Just checking that leak," said Bob as he got up, rubbing his hands on the thighs of his blue overalls. "We had a problem. Maggie's got a big sales meeting at eleven to seal a deal, and the entry door to the Pioneers Room was jammed."

"So, couldn't she just clinch the deal in another room?"

"All Maggie's sales stuff was already set up in there, there was no time to set up replacements."

"Bloody hell. If a balls up costs her a sale we'll know about it."

"It's sorted, I stayed back. It wasn't the lock, so the only way was to bust the thing open and re-fit. Pig of a job. Two of Ron's guys came up and mucked in, and Salvo dropped everything to get the nibbles set up last minute."

"Where did you get the part?"

"One of Ron's people, that tall guy that always wins at the darts. Apparently this same thing happened years ago, he knew some old style fitting that will hold it for now."

"So I can definitely tell Maggie it's sorted?"

"Yep," said Bob, "she can break in and out all she wants."

"Who can?" The voice belonged to a smartly dressed mixed race woman in her 40s, standing very upright and correctly.

"Ah talk of the devil," said Slade. "Yep Maggie, the Pioneers Room is sorted."

"Brilliant."

"Bob here, plus some of Ron and Salvo's boys mucked in to perform one of their usual miracles."

"Ah Bob, as always the diamond," said Maggie patting Bob on the arm. "Look, I've gotta dash..."

Arnie gave her a parting smile, but Maggie just looked straight through him.

And a good morning to you too.

"Good," said Slade, noting the completed task on his clipboard. "I didn't fancy our chances of finding a firm to sort that one out in time. Right then Arnie..."

"Can I have an ARFA form please..."

"A what!"

"An ARFA form. For my bucket."

"Your bucket?"

"Yeah, Ron said I needed an ARFA form for it. I'd say my bucket seems ok, but..."

Slade laughed. "Arnie forget the bucket. Ron was winding you up...."

"Eh?"

"Your induction, he was getting you at it."

"At it...?"

"ARFA form, get it? Halfa form. In the old days I'd have now suckered you with half a sheet of paper to fill in and take back to him. I suppose I was meant to sign it?"

"Yeah."

"And did he ask you about different types of buckets or mops too?"

"Buckets..."

"...a load of old crap. He's only got one kind."

"Oh right."

"We did away with these pranks years ago, but Ron is old school. This is nothing, you should have seen how they had me going on my first day."

9

"Oh!"

"Listen, next time you're down there, kid him that the soap holders are hazardous or something and he'll love it. But get this. Ron is a top supplies guy, his team sort out the gear for all our global sites on a shoestring. So joke with him, but don't try to take liberties with them down there..."

Arnie shuffled his feet. *Pissing bucket assessment indeed...*

"Right," interrupted Bob putting his wrench into a toolbox, "that rad is sorted too so I'm off to catch up on some sleep." He began heading for the lift.

"You look knackered Bob, book it as overtime. And well done."

"I'm on days the rest of the week. Is it alright if I take it as time off in lieu and finish a little earlier on Friday instead? It's the youngest one's birthday and I'm out of annual leave?"

"Sure, be good to have you out of my hair for a few hours."

"Thanks Jim," said Bob entering the lift, "I mean James!"

"Get the hell out of here!"

Arnie ducked as a hurled clipboard smashed against the closing lift doors.

* * *

That evening Arnie walked out of the Albion building and strolled up the long pebbled path that cut through Albion's large front lawn. He had stayed late on his first day to help make a good impression. It had been a long day.

But a happy one.

As the path approached the street Arnie ventured onto the grass and sprang up a little raised green bank that ran around the lawn's edge to mark Albion's boundary. From atop of his little waist-high perch he tapped out a text to

Lucy to let her know he was working again at last, and that the first day had gone well. *Just to let her know he's not the failure she said he was.*

He hit 'Send.'

Hopefully tomorrow would go well, the thought this job wouldn't stick nagged at him. 'Last in, first out' was a mantra he had grown up with. He rubbed his legs, he had got stuck in today and some muscles he'd long forgotten were aching.

He stared back at the building for a few moments in the fading spring daylight. The lights of nine floors of Albion's HQ shone back at him. The block was essentially a cube with an art deco façade and external steps going up to the raised entrance. In the foreground was the most immaculate front lawn Arnie had ever seen, dissected by the pebbled path winding its way up the middle.

It was some sight. To think the happy few that worked in that building were supporting global sites around the world from Alaska to the Bay of Bengal, and all thanks to those that had built this company in years past. And hopefully he too would get the chance to do his little bit here. Tomorrow he would set that alarm early.

He skipped down the other side of the grassy bank and onto the pavement, and whistled as he headed up the street towards the bus stop, and home.

Devoux stood at the head of the boardroom table and flicked his bright yellow tie. "The world is changing," he said, letting the words hang for a moment. "Albion must modernise."

Through his rimless glasses he surveyed the countless old portraits of his predecessors that adorned the oak panelled boardroom.

"You have the briefing notes," he said to the three faces before him as he sat down. "We must be able to respond faster to new challenges. I will not let this company slip on my watch."

The other three stared back in silence.

"Mr Friedman," Devoux said, addressing one of the two other men who had started with him today. "I believe you have already put feelers out?"

A tall balding man in his fifties and wearing a dark suit opened a file. "Early soundings show a healthy level of interest in operating our overseas sites, rent them from us, buy them, whatever it takes to lighten our staff burden." Matthew Friedman smiled as he ran his index finger around his white collar, "In fact, it looks like we could create a bit of an auction."

"Encouraging. And Mr Yates?" Devoux turned toward the man in his forties with thick dark hair who had also started today. "Your initial assessment?"

Gary Yates adjusted his large glasses and put down the tablet he had been looking at. Unusual to be called by his real name, he had got used to his nickname of 'Gates' due to his IT prowess. "Our analysis shows that there's huge scope for IT solutions to replace people here. We can devise new systems to suit the demands of this company very quickly."

"Good."

"But in the meantime, we already have a cutting edge payroll system linked to staff performance that can be rolled out at once."

"Do it. And Mrs Rutherford, have you any observations?"

Greta Rutherford, an older woman in a two-piece tweed suit and a single strand pearl necklace stared back at him. "You already have my response in the pre-handover briefing report. For the record I want to repeat this here. Over the many years I served under the Hudson Brothers we overcame everything thrown at us. We saw off all competition ranging from old giants to new kids on the block. We are a winner, we are in profit, and forecasts are good. So all I say is, 'don't throw the baby out with the bath water'. My finer points will be presented in a further report."

Devoux glared at her through rimless glasses and squinted eyes. "Right," he said as he turned back to the others, "Mr Yates earn your corn, and go ahead with rolling out that new payroll system."

"I'm on it Mr. Devoux."

"Mr Friedman, firm up some offers on offloading our overseas sites, I want outsourcing to be the go-to option."

"A pleasure Mr Devoux."

"And Mr Friedman, I took a walk around this building earlier, we need to modernise quickly. And if we must waste money paying so many people, get some personal accountability going on, some edge. It's too cosy. And find ways to trim back, and I mean do it yesterday.

"Outsource, outsource, outsource."

TUESDAY

The next morning Arnie bounced into work early. There was a delay getting in as up ahead Roger and the other concierges were working with calm military efficiency to check some assorted packages with a scanner. That was reassuring, can't be too careful these days.

"Good morning Mr Smeggins, you're very spritely today."

"Things to do Roger, you look very busy, you have a good day too."

Arnie checked his phone one last time before starting work. Nothing back from Lucy, not even a thumbs up emoji. *Oh well.*

Exiting the lift at Floor 8, he popped his phone away and glanced around to get his bearings. Ahead of him Slade's door was closed as was the big wooden door to the right marked *'Traders' Offices'*. Between the two was the narrow corridor to the small locker room they had given him to keep his clothes and trolley. He quickly nipped in, pulled on his overalls and within moments he had wheeled his trolley into the lobby. It was time to get cracking. He opened the cleaning cupboard near the lift and balked.

It was empty.

Strange.

Ron said they were all restocked first thing each morning. No matter, he would grab some stuff from the cupboard on the floor below. Ron's staff must have forgotten this one. He went down a level, turned the key and jolted.

What the...?

It was empty too. This sure was odd, even on his second day he could tell that, and it was setting back his early start. Arnie tried the next floor down.

It was empty too.

He stood up, best not waste time finding somebody to ask, and he didn't really know many people yet. And best not to bother Jim Slade. No, he'd head down with his trolley to sort this out with Ron. Arnie called the lift and whistled a tune, at least today he could give Ron as good as he got after this cock up.

I'll give him his pissing bucket assessment.

The lift doors opened in the Basement. Arnie blinked twice as he wheeled his trolley out.

What the hell...?

The main lights were off. He peered through the half-light. Dull emergency lamps were now semi-illuminating the ghostly corridors. It was quieter too, kinda eerie, and the smell was different, a strange kind of unlived in smell. Only the whirring of the building's plant was the same. Gingerly he advanced, like an intruder in a museum at midnight.

He reached the open space and peered through the gloom, the place was empty. Above him the *'Supplies'* sign was squeaking on its two rusty chains as it swayed in the chilly draft that blew up the corridor. All else was silent. The trollies and boxes were gone, and Ron's hatch was sealed. Arnie approached an official looking sign on Ron's hatch.

'For all Supplies contact the
Granwick Provisions Company.'

There was also a web address and a phone number. What the hell was this all about? Arnie pulled out his mobile, he would have to contact Jim now, although he might not get a signal down here.

A click on the line and he did. "Hey Jim, Arnie here, sorry to trouble you on my second day but all the cleaning cupboards are empty. I came down to see Ron and he's missing too, just a sign saying contact Granwick."

"Aye lad, seems the news didn't get to you this morning. Ron and his team are gone. Supplies has been outsourced. You must place an online order with the Granwick Provisions Company who have the deal with us now. They deliver in two hours. Go to Finance to get an order number to set up your own Granwick account.

"Oh ok ... and er I have to set up my own account you say?"

"Oh yeah, that's the other thing. All staff must order separately now too, no central supply anymore. New system to monitor how much bleach and so on each of you uses. So get the lock changed on one of the cupboards too. Put your name on it to make sure that from now on that cupboard becomes your own store. All staff will only be able to use their personal allowance from their own cupboard, no matter which part of the building they're working in."

"So where's Ron?"

"Pensioned off."

Arnie peered at the hatch in the gloom, another smaller

piece of paper was pinned to the hatch at an angle with a hand scrawled message. "Hey Jim, there's another sign down here."

"Ahh is there now. What does it say?"

Arnie moved closer. "It says: *'Gone Fishing, for the purposes of. Ron.'*

Slade gave a sad laugh. "That sounds like our Ron alright. You know he only talked like that as a joke. He was sending up what people thought he should sound like. A shame he's gone, he was the best supplies guy around. So do you know what to do?"

"I think so. Before I can clean the toilets this morning I need to go to Accounts Department, get an order number, set up my account, log in, place an order with Granwick, then I guess pick the stuff up from Roger in the lobby when it's delivered in two hours."

"You've got it. Good."

"So that's why Roger's people were held up scanning lots of parcels this morning?"

"That's right. Now before doing all that come and see me, I've something important to tell you. Change of plans."

Arnie arrived up at the Building Services door a few minutes later. It was open so he edged in. Inside was not Jim's office as he had expected but a large open space. Over to the left was the open door to Slade's actual office, and to the right was a long row of cupboards and shelving with various tools hanging up. Straight ahead, side by side were two small work cubbyholes made of hardboard and glass partitions, with their open plan sides facing Arnie. The names *'Bob'* and *'Alison'* were above each one.

Arnie nodded to Bob who was swearing at a laptop on his little desk in his cubbyhole. "Who's Alison?" Arnie asked.

"My co-worker. She's on leave, back Friday," said Bob frowning at his screen.

"Hey Arnie," hollered Slade from his office as he put down his phone, "that was quick. Great! Come in here."

Arnie crossed the room and hovered at the entrance to Slade's office.

"Well come in, come in, sit down, sit down. And leave the door open."

"Sorry, thanks, sorry."

"So, are you settling in ok?"

"Yeah fine thanks."

"Before I forget, they're changing the payroll over to a new IT system, so go to Human Resources to sign a form. Make sure you do it soon. Got that, good."

"Sure Jim, will do."

"Good. Now then Arnie. The world has changed since you arrived yesterday, do you know what outsourcing means?"

"Not really."

"Basically it means we pay outside firms to do the work that our own people once did."

"Oh right, shall I clean the toilets now?" Arnie raised himself.

"Hang on Arnie, sit back down."

Arnie did so.

"With Ron's team gone I've been given an added role. I will have to be the Albion guy here that liaises with this Granwick Company, make sure they're doing what we pay them for, tell them what we want, that sort of thing. You follow?"

"He's got a long new title Arnie, it's called Buildings Manager and Chief Contracts Client Manager," chirped Bob from his cubbyhole, "he'll need a bigger door to put all his new nameplates on."

"No work to do Bob?"

Bob trudged out.

"Now Arnie, the truth is that with this outsourcing we're suddenly a bit stretched, as am I. To get to the point, I have an offer for you. Maggie has a huge convention in the Chartwell Suite on Saturday on Floor 6, an annual thing for some of our clients and some possible new ones. But it needs a bit of spit and polish over the next three or four days to get the place gleaming. So I'm going to ask if you want to take it on. Do you know the Chartwell yet?"

"Kind of. I saw inside when I did the lobby there yesterday..."

"Right. Well basically you'll have seen the builder's dust dotted about. That's left over from some renovations we had done last week to spruce it up for this convention."

"Yeah I noticed ..."

"Right, but before agreeing, here's the key thing. You will need to manage yourself, you know schedule your own work, use your initiative. From today with Ron's team gone I'm gonna be way too tied up with this new role liaising with Granwick to supervise you, and I'll probably be out of the building quite a lot. From what I saw yesterday, you're well capable of managing yourself anyway. Truth is Arnie, previously I could get some of Ron's people to muck in on a bit of overtime if we were a bit tight, but with this outsourcing Albion has lost all that flexibility."

"Jim, I..."

"Look, I know it's only your second day, so say no if you want to, and I'll have to get a firm in to do it. But there'll be a nice bonus in it for you for getting Chartwell shipshape, and the company will appreciate it."

Arnie shifted in his seat, taking it in. He could hear Lucy laughing at the thought of this *'useless heap of a nobody'* taking on responsibility. That Chartwell Suite was sure in a bit of a state but getting it sorted by Saturday should be a breeze. The bonus was nice, but more than that, this was his chance to make a good impression in his first week. He had to keep this job.

Slade extended his hand to clinch the deal.

Arnie only needed half a second more to think about it. He shook Slade's hand and the words emerged on their own...

"Albion can rely on me."

"Splendid!"

* * *

A few minutes later the metallic lift voice announced; "Floor 2 Accounts and Finance," and Arnie soon found himself waiting at a 'Staff Queries' counter. Time to order his stuff so he could get cracking. He rang the bell and waited.

A woman emerged. "Oh my God, Arni-e-e-e!"

"Hey Sue, what the....!" Arnie flushed, fancy his former neighbour working here. "My, you're looking great."

"And you too Arnie, so you work here now too?"

"Yep. Started yesterday as janitor..."

"Wonderful."

"How's Lucy?"

Arnie shuffled his feet. "We separated a few months back, she moved out."

"Oh I'm sorry. Any chance you two might..."

"I doubt it, but who knows..."

"Oh well, it's great to see you…"

"You too. Look I need an order number to set up some kind of account to get my stuff."

"Ah sure, the Granwick contract. You do know you'll have your own order number on this now. So go easy, it's so that they can track what each of you are using too."

Arnie nodded, it was as Slade had said.

"Got your payroll number?"

"Er no, I've not had a pay slip yet."

"Ah…I need that pay number to process your order," Sue stared at the screen and tapped some keys. "Nope, it says it's a required field; won't let me do anything without that. No problem Arnie, nip upstairs to Human Resources, they'll let you know your payroll number, then come back here and I'll help you set up your account with Granwick."

"All this before I can clean the toilets?"

Sue smiled. "Perhaps it's progress Arnie?"

"Sure, back soon Sue."

"Oh Arnie…"

"What?"

"…when you're up in Human Resources we all need to sign a new staff payroll form today. I just did mine."

"Yeah I heard that from Mr Slade."

"Be good working with you Arnie. Welcome to Albion."

"Thanks Sue."

At the lift Arnie's mind was spinning. Strange how he already felt so tired and he hadn't done anything yet. Damn it, Human Resources and Granwick could wait, he really needed to get cracking without all this time wasting. He was responsible for the Chartwell now, supposed to use his initiative. And he was out of stuff. He stood by the lift and rubbed his chin. Surely Bob would have some gear somewhere he could use until this account thing was sorted tomorrow.

Arnie found Bob in his cubbyhole, still hurling curses at his laptop. Maggie was just gliding in.

"Hey Maggie," said Bob looking up. "If you're looking for Jim, he just got called out. Something went wrong over at Granwick."

Maggie gave Bob a smirk-cum-smile and placed a wrapped object, obviously a bottle on his desk. "Just a little thank you for yesterday..."

"Oh Maggie there's no need..."

"I think there is. We closed the deal and it's a big one. You didn't have to stay back and volunteer."

"I couldn't possibly take that," grinned Bob, grabbing up the bottle and hugging it to his chest.

"You know," said Maggie half to herself and half to Bob. "Somehow it really helps to use that Pioneers Room, we always seem to clinch deals in there. Maybe the vibe of them pioneer days with all those grand old photos brings us luck."

"Not my field really. But I'd hazard a guess it's because people can actually walk through a door that opens."

Maggie chuckled.

"And Salvo says it's his dips that win the deals."

"I'll take that bottle back if you're not careful. Listen see you around, and thanks again, you're a blond cockney diamond."

"Diamond will do, thanks."

Arnie smiled at Maggie as she departed, but she just ignored him again.

Huh!

"Damn and shit!" Bob thumped the table. "It's timed me out!"

Arnie jumped back.

"What bollocks! Now I'll have to log in and start over. I was only talking to Maggie for a minute. Bloody Granwick crap! I've got two radiators to fix, a broken window frame in the street level Gents and I need to order some lubricant. I've been an hour trying to set up this bloody account. Yesterday I'd have done half a dozen jobs by now. Sorry man, letting off steam, how you doing Arnie?"

"All's good thanks, except I've got no stuff. Got any here I could use?"

"Hey man yesterday of course I would have, but today is different. We all have our own cupboards now."

"Sure I understand."

"Sorry I feel terrible."

"No I get it."

Arnie started walking away.

"Hey Arnie come back. Look, this is total bollocks. There's my cupboard over there, it's open. Take whatever you need. Just make sure you replace it later this week, otherwise my figures will be flying over Mars."

"Thanks Bob. Sorry, everything is new to me."

"You're doing great buddy. If my cupboard's locked just leave it on my or Alison's desk. Blimey I'm already saying 'my' isn't it crazy how this crap gets into your bones so quick."

Arnie reached in and started taking some stuff.

Bob leaned out of his cubbyhole. "Hey Arnie, best you also grab some silver polish for the staff trophy cabinet. It's by the Pioneers Room."

"Yeah I saw that yesterday."

"Let that slip and Jim will be on your case. Some of them cups go back forty years."

"Yeah I saw them."

Bob lit up. "Hey, with that tall guy in Supplies gone that darts cup could be mine this year. Do you play darts, bowls, anything?"

"Not much for a while."

"Put your name down for a works team. Good way to meet folks, helps us workwise too to know faces. When top brass do it they call it networking, when we do it they call it loafing."

"Yeah I will."

Out in the lobby and armed with supplies, Arnie took stock. He had lost most of the morning chasing his tail but thanks to Bob he could now start work today. He would head for them bloody toilets near the Chartwell Suite then set to work on the suite itself. He would get that whole floor gleaming for Saturday, they'd see. If he was to keep this job it was time to get some work done.

Human Resources and their bloody payroll form could wait.

* * *

That evening Arnie strode up the path on his way home. He had made a good start today, but the Chartwell Suite needed lots of love to get it ready for Saturday. With a fair wind he should be able to crack it, and maybe with a few days to spare. That would surely stand him in good stead, he'd lost so many jobs through no fault of his own, redundancy, firm closure, cuts, restructuring, everything.

Hopefully not this time.

Near the path's end he skipped onto the lawn and up the little raised grassy bank. He puffed his chest out and got out his phone to text Lucy the news. Maybe her phone was broken, that could explain why she hadn't replied to his texts.

He hit 'Send' and gazed at the Albion Building, the nine floors of lights shining back at him in the fading spring daylight. It was good to be part of something again.

But odd that with Ron's team gone, the floor that couldn't be seen was now in darkness.

Devoux glared at Greta Rutherford from his perch at the head of the boardroom table. "I'll come to you in a moment Mrs Rutherford. Mr Friedman, progress report."

"I am delighted to report the successful outsourcing of Supplies. No operational disruption at all, in fact I'd say we are already more flexible and agile. The owner of Granwick is an old friend of mine, solid company, they'll be an excellent partner."

"Cut faster Mr Friedman."

"Music to my ears Mr Devoux."

"And Mr Yates, I asked for IT solutions to help us modernise."

Yates coughed and adjusted his large glasses. "The new payroll system was tested today. It is good to go. Our Human Resources staff will be trained on the transfer tomorrow morning. It is linked to new staff appraisals and performance targets that are designed to get the maximum potential from each employee."

"Good. The vision is clear in your papers. We will be a modernised finance and trading company based on streamlined core functions. We will remove barriers to performance. In the world that's coming, it's the only way. So get outsourcing Mr Friedman. Which brings me to your report Mrs Rutherford." He slid a document along the table at her, "You promised me a further full briefing."

"That is it."

Devoux removed his rimless glasses and laid them in front of him. "I wanted forecasts, risks, and strategies to tackle those risks."

"You already had all that before you got here."

"Not on modernisation I haven't. How we find the fastest way to become streamlined so we'll be able to cope with future threats. Instead you give me froth about good industrial relations, goodwill, reputation capital, environmental awards, and so forth. The *world is changing, old thinking will kill us. Have you any idea how fast they are moving in the Far East? I repeat, our aim is to be lean, modern, agile."*

"We are agile. I want to place this formally on record now. In my twenty five years here we have always reformed as needed. We overcame everything thrown at us, price fluctuations, market changes, wars, market crashes, pandemics, stupid government regulations, almost sound government regulations, hostile govern-ments, and in every quarter of the globe. And yes emerging competitors. We've knocked them all out of the ring. We've adapted. The figures are good, the projections are sound, and the key asset that others can't touch is our workforce."

Devoux cut in. "It was once. Maybe. Perhaps. Who knows? Who cares? But now it's an albatross around our necks. There's a tough wind coming from the Far East. Global challenges. We must grasp the nettle and reform. No time for sentimentality."

"It's not sentimentality, it's proven sound business," said Greta Rutherford closing her report.

Devoux turned his head. "Mr Yates, get those new staff appraisals and performance indicators going at once. To survive we must modernise quickly."

"It will be up and running tomorrow Mr Devoux."

WEDNESDAY

Arnie was loving his job.

The next morning the rain was incessant. Arnie joined the other early birds under the outside canopy shaking down their wet umbrellas. There seemed to be a slight delay going in.

"Somebody has sounded the fire alarm," explained a tall Sikh guy in a sharp suit, his voice just audible above the patter of spring rain on the awning above them. "False alarm by the looks of it. No worries, Roger and his team seem to have it all in hand."

Within a few minutes the barriers opened and Arnie walked inside. Roger and the others seemed calmly unfazed by the whole thing and the show was on the road again as people flooded into work.

"Morning Mr Smeggins, you have a good day now sir."

"Morning Roger, busy one for you already eh?"

"Just keeping us on our toes as it were sir."

The first hour flew by as Arnie cleaned the lobbies on some lower floors that were on his roster, then he went up to attack the Chartwell Suite for the rest of the day.

Right, time to do battle!

He surveyed the leftover builders' dust. The carpet in the main suite would take several goes to get right, the lobby floor needed sorting, and these toilets sure want a good long scrubbing. He reached into the basket at the foot of his trolley. Damn he'd used the last of the stuff he'd borrowed from Bob. He straightened up with the cloth in his hand, so what to do now? He spoke aloud to himself to get a better grip of it all.

"*Right, before I can get to work on these toilets I need more stuff, and with Ron gone I need to order that from Granwick. But I can't do that until Human Resources. No that's wrong. I mean I can't do that until Sue in Finance sets me up an account with Granwick and gets it delivered downstairs to Roger, for it then to be kept in my own locked cupboard, and Sue can't do that for me without my payroll number, and she can't do that because I need to first go and get one from Human Resources. Right, I think that's it.*"

He sighed, it sure was much easier to get stuff done on Monday. He headed down to Human Resources on Floor 3. A sign greeted him...

'Human Resources closed, will reopen in a few hours. Staff training on new IT system.'

Shit! Right, he'd go and tell Jim Slade. Oh hang on, he was meant to work unsupervised, use his own initiative. And what if he and Bob were not meant to swop stuff, what with all this personal accountability or whatever they were calling it. But on the other hand he had work to do today, and he had to pay Bob back too.

Shit and more shit!

There was only one thing for it. He would nip out to a

hardware store, pay for the stuff himself, and get cracking. He just had to keep this job. Tomorrow he'd sort out all this admin. Somehow.

Down at the entrance Roger and the guys were over in the corner being spoken to by some guys in suits. Odd.

Arnie emerged into the rain and pulled his coat over his head. He headed down three blocks to a store, picked up some cleaning stuff, and dashed back through the heavy shower laden with a big bag. He reached the entrance, wiped the rain from his face, and stopped dead.

What the...?

"What do you want?" said a huge brick outhouse of a guy with an earpiece and a mic who looked look like he was guarding a seedy downtown night club at two in the morning.

"To come in. I work here."

"Pass," he said abruptly, failing to look at Arnie and chewing on his gum.

"Pardon?"

"I said pass or no entry."

Arnie looked at the stranger on the door with the Albion crest on one side of his jacket and some awful logo on the other. "Er I left it inside by mistake, I only just popped out. Where's Roger? He'll vouch for me."

The burglar alarm sounded, making Arnie jump.

"Hey," said the outhouse to another bruiser, "go sort that damn alarm out will ya ... and hey you," he yelled across the lobby, "yeah you," he was pointing at a third bouncer, "who the hell is that other guy over there by the lift, you're supposed to be watching who comes in. Go and check him out, I can only do one thing at once."

"Don't agg' me man, I'm busy here."

The outhouse eventually turned back to Arnie. "Now

your pass or no entry. Final." His fingers went to his mouth and a loud shrill whistle to a guy across the lobby made Arnie cover his nearest ear.

"Hey mister, wrong door! Mister! Oi! This way!"

Arnie rubbed his ear and trudged back outside into the rain laden with the bag of cleaning gear. If only he hadn't left his phone inside he could call Jim. What a nightmare. He'd managed to get some extra strong stuff for a stubborn stain near the Floor 6 lift, but now he couldn't even get in Floor 1. A moment standing in the drizzle and the answer hit him.

Hadn't Bob said yesterday that he hadn't yet been able to fix a broken window frame in a ground level Gents.

Around the back of the building Arnie found it. The letter box shaped window with the frame half hanging off was a bit too high to climb into, but Arnie soon found a few discarded crates that he piled up. He threw the bag of cleaning stuff in, hoping nobody was going to get a shock during their call of nature.

No yelps, good.

Arnie hopped onto the crates and engineered himself up. Levering his first leg in he heard a rip, damn, he had torn his new Albion overalls. Almost horizontally, he squeezed to get in, Lucy had sure been right about his pot belly. Holding in his gut, he managed to just get his torso through the gap, then the trailing leg as he rolled around and dropped down via the toilet bowl to the floor. Once in the cubicle, he wiped his hands on his overalls, gathered up his supplies and peered out of the door.

The rest of the Gents was empty.

With a huge sigh he exited the toilets unseen.

In the corridor the burglar alarm was more piercing. Further up some Albion staff were signalling to each other that all was ok, while another new outhouse was running around in a panic shouting something. After a few more moments the alarm went silent.

A sense of relief filled Arnie. He left the chaos and went up and replaced the stuff on Bob's desk. Then clutching the rest of his bag of supplies he headed for Human Resources still dripping with rainwater. This time the door was open, he walked in and immediately shot a spark of recognition.

"Hey buddy, you're looking even wetter than you did earlier," it was the tall Sikh guy in the smart suit that he had met at the entrance this morning. He was wearing the name badge Sandeep.

"Sure is a foul day," Arnie answered.

Sandeep chuckled above the buzz of phones and busy chatter behind him. "You just come in after all this time, or have we got some pretty leaky bathrooms you're cleaning?"

"Very funny."

"Only kidding."

"You were in early for an office guy this morning."

"Switching over to new payroll systems and staff appraisals. I've never had so much to do. I had to prep for the training this morning. Speaking of which, have you signed the consent form yet to transfer your details onto this new staff IT system?"

"No."

"You must be the last one. Here take this form and drop it back as soon as you can, very important. Now what can I do for you...?"

A few minutes later Arnie left the wise cracking Sandeep in Human Resources and punched the air in triumph. He had repaid Bob and now he had his payroll number. Great! Funny how he had such a feeling of achievement.

He was on a roll, and he hadn't done any work yet.

Now to get this payroll number to Sue in Finance to get the account sorted out, then he could at last order his own supplies, and then finally start doing something about those Chartwell Suite toilets.

Why was it suddenly so difficult to do any bloody work?

Clutching his payroll number for Sue like a winning lottery ticket he headed for Accounts on Floor 2. The lift opened.

What the...?

Arnie double checked to see he had the right floor. Yep this was Floor 2. But everything was different. Not only were the lights mostly out but it was deathly quiet. He approached the spot where he had rung the bell to see Sue yesterday. There was a sign on the wall.

'For all Financial Services contact
Burridge and Perkins Accounts Co.'

He scratched his head, what the hell's happening now? He put down his bag of cleaning gear and fumbled for his phone. "Hey Jim, Arnie here, look I'm so sorry to bother you but I'm starting to get a bit confused. I need to set up my Granwick Account."

"Haven't you done that yet?"

"I didn't have a payroll number to do it and..."

"Never mind..."

"And I've come down to Finance to see Sue and there's a notice."

"Yes we're using Burridge and Perkins for all financial support now."

"So where's Sue?"

"Made redundant with all her team. Shame really, she

was a rock in this place. Had lots of offers to work elsewhere for higher pay, but she stayed loyal to Albion for years."

"That's too bad, I knew Sue from way back. So how do I get my cleaning stuff?"

"What you have to do is..." at that the burglar alarm sounded again. Slade held until it cleared, "I was saying security is also outsourced so tell them downstairs that your stuff ..." the burglar alarm started up again, then a moment's reprieve, "got that ...ood. Arnie you still there?..."

"Yeah."

"Yeah spot of bother with the alarms Arnie. Get yourself here and we'll sort everything. Hurry though, I have to be over at Granwick all afternoon sorting out their... *beep, beep* ... Arnie, you'll have to excuse me I've another call coming through from Granwick now, they must want something. See you in a minute."

"Will do Jim."

Arnie walked to the lobby and called the lift. Things were changing and not for the better, Roger's people had seemed to handle a fire alarm going off without any fuss at all this morning. He gazed at the list of floors beside the lift while he waited, it was getting harder to keep up with things.

The lift doors slid open and Arnie balked. Stone-faced Maggie was already travelling up, busy looking at her phone.

Arnie gave a hesitant mini nod as he stepped in, placed his bag of cleaning stuff on the floor, and stared at the wall to avoid eye contact. His eyes darted around the ceiling, then at a different wall, then the ceiling again but at different spots this time. Then he read the '*Max 16 Persons*' sign for the third time.

A sudden jolt rocked him as the lift made a whining

noise and juddered to a halt between floors. Arnie swallowed, he was running out of lift wall to look at. He dropped his head to survey his feet, then bent down and did a fake inspection of what was inside his bag of cleaning stuff.

After a while Maggie looked up from her phone, "You'd best press that lift alarm button above your head."

Arnie did as he was instructed and waited for a voice to come on the intercom. After a buzzing noise a voice crackled.

"Yeah?"

Arnie placed his mouth to the speaker. "Hi, we're in Lift 2 and we're stuck, probably somewhere around Floors 4 and 5 I think."

"Hang on," the voice replied, "one of the guys has messed with something."

"When can you get us moving?" said Maggie moving forward and speaking into the grill.

"I dunno."

"Well find out!"

"How?"

"Listen," Maggie said into the speaker. "In half an hour I have a meeting with a valued client of ours who means a lot to this place, so whatever else you're doing, I suggest you focus on getting me to my office. Understand?"

"Is it?"

"Yes it bloody well is!"

"Cool."

The voice returned after another adjournment. "They say it will be 20 minutes."

Maggie slumped back against the wall, threw her head back and sighed.

Arnie suddenly felt for her. "You alright?"

"Fine thanks. My God you're soaking wet!"

"Long story."

"And your trousers are torn!"

Arnie looked down at his exposed knee. "Oh damn, sorry, I had to climb in through a window."

"Should I ask? I am a head of department here you know."

Arnie gulped. "I sort of forgot my pass, and I only went out for ten minutes because I needed to ...er .... I mean it was something to do with work, not personal and ...er.... well I didn't have my pass or phone with me, and so I couldn't get back in with these new security people, and I wanted to get on with my work, and um ... well there's a Gents toilet.. and that's it really."

Damn, how to make an even worse impression in 10 seconds.

Maggie smiled as if miles away. "You know this new security firm have only just got here and already they've messed with the burglar alarm, now he says they've done something to the lifts."

"New firm?"

"Roger and the other concierge fellas are gone."

"I kinda got that but..."

"Our building security and reception is now outsourced to a company called Muscorva Security. I'm not sure the lifts should even be part of their remit."

Arnie bit his tongue. He was new here and he certainly wasn't going to criticise anything or anybody.

"Anyway my name's Maggie," she said.

"I'm Arnie. I've seen you around."

She stared back blankly.

"I was in Bob's office yesterday," he explained.

"Oh yes of course. You're the guy that was hanging around up there. Are you new?"

"Started Monday."

"It's not always like this here. Welcome."

"Thanks."

At that her phone went off. At least they had a signal in here. Maggie fumbled in her pocket, glanced at the screen, and seemed to decline a call as she popped the phone back into her pocket.

"Nice ring tune," Arnie said, "Bessie Smith's Nobody Knows You."

"My God that's right! Nobody knows that song, and the few that do always call it by the cover by Eric Clapton."

"Ah dear ol' Bessie. But you know I prefer the old Scrapper Blackwell version with guitar. Probably his best solo without Leroy Carr's piano."

"No, it has to be Bessie on that one, more earthy."

"True, but I prefer Scrapper's different lyrics in one verse."

"Ah you're a proper lover of old blues I see?"

"Sure am."

"You know, it's a dream of mine to write a book about some of the blues greats one day."

"I'd like to read that. Me, I collect old blues on vinyl. I have some early stuff by Bessie too..."

The intercom hissed again. "Er there's a bit of a problem it will be an hour."

"An hour!" screeched Maggie. "What the hell did I tell you."

"We have to get the firm in to fix it, they're sending for an engineer innit."

"This is outrageous."

"Sorry lady."

"Don't you dare call me lady ever again."

"Cool."

Maggie sighed and hit the speaker on her phone.

"Hasna, look I'm stuck in our lift. I know, don't ask. Now then, are you able to step into my meeting with Polar and Mason this morning? Briefing notes are on file."

"Sure Maggie, but I've been dragged out of the building. I'm at Burridge and Perkins right now, they've muddled the payment lines for our entire promo budget, I'm at their place trying to straighten it out. Then I need to meet with Jim about Saturday."

"Sorry Hasna, Jim will be out at Granwick all afternoon, they've got supply problems, he's being dragged over there again."

"Damn, I needed to see him. And I really need to be prepping for Saturday's sales pitch Maggie."

"Don't forget we also have to start on the new staff appraisals today..."

"Oh hell."

"Plus we have our new performance indicators and targets to reset."

"Maggie..."

"And then we must link the two for each staff member, and then arrange one-to-one sessions with each of them. Then for each one we have to write up a review linked to key perform..."

"Maggie I can't see how I will have time..."

"Hasna..."

"I've already lost half the bloody morning here with these Burridge and Perkins guys trying to sort out their payments cock up. Sue's team would have done this blindfolded. And now I can't get to meet Jim this afternoon. Sorry Maggie, it's just..."

"I hear you Hasna.."

"And I should at some stage be finalising Brunel ready for...."

"Hasna forget Project Brunel. It'd be impossible to operate it with our Supplies and Finance gone. We're gonna have to scrap all new business ideas that involved our other departments..."

"After all that work! Is there not even a faint chance of salvaging something from it Maggie? Say with Granwick and Burridge and Perkins helping us to..."

"Realistically Hasna, none. They're only working to tight contracts. To operate Brunel we'd need our own people working day to day with us to deal with..."

"What a complete bloody waste. Look sorry Maggie, sure I can drop everything here and grab a cab back if it's urgent?"

"Yes, Hasna if you could that would be best."

"No problem."

"And Hasna..."

"Yeah I'm still here..."

"Don't tell Polar and Mason I'm stuck in one of our own bloody lifts, we'll look ridiculous, tell them I'm on a flight that's been delayed or something. Thanks."

Maggie sighed and put her phone away, and slowly slid her back down the wall until she was sitting on the floor with her knees up.

Arnie sat down too on the other side of the lift and ran his hand through his thinning damp hair.

"You know," she sighed, "some days like Monday I'm winning big new deals for Albion, but most days winning is just about keeping the customers we have happy. That's the biggest part of this job. That's what Saturday is all about, and the meeting I just handed over to Hasna, my deputy. Hard to do that from in here."

"I'm just trying to get Chartwell shipshape to help you do that... in my own little way of course."

Maggie smiled. "There's nothing little about it Arnie. I'm sure it will all be nice and gleaming by Saturday."

"Hum, well yeah, it's kinda coming along."

"Great! Albion is counting on you." Another smile broke across her face, "Right then Arnie, to pass the time, name five of your favourite Bessie Smith tracks?"

* * *

That evening Arnie walked across the lobby on his way out. There was no late shift concierge to bid him a cheery good night, just one bruiser at the entrance with a spider tattoo on his neck staring at his phone. The two men ignored each other as Arnie filed out.

Arnie switched on his phone, still nothing from Lucy. Oh well, maybe she's busy. Best not trouble her again so soon. He would grab himself a takeaway tonight, funny how he was so exhausted and yet had done so little of his job today.

Somehow things were slipping. It was well past lunchtime when they had freed them from the lift, and by then Jim had already left for Granwick so Arnie was unable to set up his account. Then Bob had told him that they had to fill out some complicated new staff self-appraisal forms, that came with reams of guidance notes about some sort of performance indicators and targets. From his early start it was late afternoon before Arnie had left his completed forms on Jim's desk, and finally got back to Chartwell.

He sighed as he walked up the path.

He had stayed late again, he really needed to make a good early impression, his job may depend on it, there are 50 ways they can fire someone if they want to. Protesting that nothing was his fault would be a non-starter. He took a deep breath, surely there was now no danger he couldn't do this Chartwell thing in time.

Was there?

But just two days to go and so much to do. Tomorrow he would arrive sharpish and get on top of things. He would let nothing stop him.

He reached the edge of the green, bounded up the grassy bank, and looked back at the proud headquarters of the Greater Albion Bay Company. Lights gleamed back at him from the ninth floor down to the third.

But the lowest two floors were now in darkness.

"I'm delighted to report that the outsourcing of supplies, security and finance have all passed off without a hitch. In fact from where I sit the service we get is as good if not better than before. And our managers are thriving in their new environment."

"Encouraging Mr Friedman," said Devoux. "Continue."

"We have kept a small core finance team to meet our legal requirements that have moved into the Executive Offices on this floor with us. All the rest are redundant, and their roles performed by our wonderful new outside partners. Overseas negotiations are at an advanced stage to unload our sites. Details are before you."

"Good. And Mr Yates?"

"HR stopped work this morning to be trained on transferring all staff details onto our new payroll system with built-in staff appraisals, performance indicators and staff targets. All are progressing well."

"We've had staff appraisals and PIs for as long as I can remember," said Greta. "But this version adds up to a very inward facing focus. A huge distraction from the...."

"...I don't see what's unreasonable about asking all staff members to fill out a form so that they each reflect upon what skills they are bringing to us, and then their line managers sitting down to match these skills to their department's performance indicators. Managers will then be empowered to set personal targets with each staff member that are referenced across a matrix of key company goals, write up individual performance plans for each of their members of staff that can feed into their training needs analysis, and use this data to inform their next departmental performance review cycle. Modernisation, Mrs Rutherford."

"...as I said, a huge inward distraction of time and energy. We've already had to cancel several promising business projects..."

"It won't distract at all, and the targeted focus will improve performance."

"Uhm."

"Repeat quarterly."

"Quarterly!"

"Shouldn't take anybody very long. Would you have us back in the dark ages, or some old kind of 1980s management by objectives type...?"

"...Mr Yates, I'm afraid this will..."

"...Right," said Devoux cutting across Greta. "Mr Friedman, you have something to add?"

"Indeed Mr Devoux," Friedman opened a file. "Our modernisation continues. Personal accountability where staff became responsible for their own supplies was just the start. From tomorrow they will all have their own devolved budgets too. Our new internal markets will allow staff to buy and sell their services from each other. Removing barriers is the mantra."

"Mrs Rutherford, anything to add?"

"Have you done an impact report on these internal markets?"

Friedman sighed and adjusted the neck of his shirt. "Of course we have. Responsibility is one impact for a start, staff will be accountable for every penny. But there's more to it than that. Much more. You watch as staff flourish with the freedom to take control. Gone are the days of them asking permission upstairs to do anything, Albion will have on the spot decision making. Staff will choose how to use their own budgets, will negotiate prices for their work, will win contracts from each other, will find the most efficient solutions, and will thrive and grow with their empowerment. So not just increased efficiency Mrs Rutherford, on the ground flexibility, responsibility, and initiative. This will unleash a new dynamism in the workplace. It's without doubt a win-win-win. You just watch."

THURSDAY

Once upon a time a janitor would be a lonesome figure entering a company building like this at such an early hour. But things had changed. In this competitive world the Greater Albion Bay Company had adapted and survived. It had expanded, resisted the onslaughts of old competitors, seen off new kids on the block, and was a world renowned success story. And all the staff who entered that building each morning knew one thing; if you want to work for a winner, you can't be a passenger.

So when Arnie arrived at the company entrance at that early hour on a spring Thursday morning, he was far from alone. He skipped up the exterior steps and through the revolving doors. He was about to go through one of the turnstiles when a gum-chewing bruiser held out an arm the size of a log.

"Wait."

Arnie stopped in his tracks, there didn't seem to be any reason to stagger the staff entering. Ahead there was some kind of heated discussion going on between two of the uniformed meatheads in the lobby. He checked his phone again while he waited, still nothing from Lucy.

Oh well silence is a message too.

"You're the new janitor aren't you," said a voice from behind, interrupting his thoughts. Arnie turned to see a Mediterranean looking middle aged guy with a broad smile.

"Yep, that's me," Arnie replied as the queue to get in started to build behind them, the murmurs of impatience growing.

"Welcome to the madhouse, the name's Salvo."

"Oh Salvo. Yeah, I've heard your name."

"All good I hope?"

"It sure was. Something about your dips being so good they win big deals."

Salvo laughed. "Just imagine what my risotto could do?"

"I'll have to order that too then," said Maggie as she caught up. "And you look better today Arnie," she added. "I thought that wet look yesterday was your fashion statement."

"Morning Maggie, yep I've got a good feeling about today."

"Glad to hear it," Maggie replied. "Counting on you to give us shining and gleaming for Saturday Arnie. And I take it you're good to go for the convention Salvo?"

"Have my dips ever let you down yet?"

Maggie gave a chuckle.

Arnie looked up, there was movement inside the lobby ahead. Whatever minor crisis had been causing the delay appeared to have been resolved. With a superior sneer the nearest bruiser waved Arnie through, and within seconds the other Albion early birds were bustling in and streaming for the lifts.

"Listen Arnie, a tip," said Salvo as they entered the

building, that smile still showing. "With this lot on the door, if you want to get in on time my team now allow themselves an extra fifteen minutes in the morning. They all want to get cracking, but that's tougher to do when getting in to work is a battle in itself."

"Yeah good shout."

"And come up to the canteen lunchtime and have a risotto to die for."

"I'd love to, you're making me hungry already."

* * *

Upstairs Arnie headed for his locker room to change into his overalls. He gazed into the mirror. Damn, what on earth did he look like with that torn knee, that hole was too big to sew up and a patch would look dreadful. If only Ron were here, he would have spare overalls by now. And another mop, how the hell could they expect him to do all this with one mop.

Right, before he could start he needed to set up his Granwick account, place his orders, and then he could spend the rest of the day uninterrupted scrubbing the Chartwell Suite for Maggie. He would have to work some to get it shining in time, but it was certainly still doable.

Oh shit, first he had to nip down and hand in his form to Sandeep. At least he didn't look like a drowned rat today.

He hurried to Floor 3, exited the lift, and stopped in his tracks.

It can't be ...

The lights were all out. Across the whole floor only the faint daylight from the windows illuminated the edges of the huge and barren office space. Behind the same counter from which sharp-suited Sandeep had helped him only yesterday was nothing but a vast sea of office-grey tiled carpet. The dozens of human resources officers beavering away at desks, segregated by the occasional office partition, were all gone. Silence had replaced the constant buzz of phones and busy chatter. Arnie was gazing at what looked like an advert for an empty office block for rent.

Damn! This could only mean one thing.

He studied the HR form in his hand, it looked important. He would be in real hot water now, he was supposed to have got this form back days ago. And worse, hadn't Sandeep said that Arnie was the only one not to hand it in.

What to do?

He could hardly ask Jim without landing himself in trouble. He folded the HR form and slid it as deeply into his pocket as he could. He pushed his keys down over it so it wouldn't fall out somewhere. Hopefully nothing would come of this.

He got out his phone, let's just push on with the day.

"Hi Jim, it's Arnie. I need to set up that Granwick account?"

"Have you still not done that yet?"

"Er I had a few problems yesterday, I'll explain, then you got called out to Granwick all afternoon."

"Look, I'm in the canteen with Bob and I need to speak to you anyway. More changes."

"OK. Oh... and by the way, I was just on Floor 3 and noticed that Sandeep and all Human Resources were gone."

"What were you doing there?"

"Er, I got out of the lift at the wrong floor, that's all."

"Right, well never mind. Look, get yourself here and I'll update you."

* * *

Arnie went straight to the canteen where he was hit by the warm smell of mocha and chocolate and the noise of busy work chatter punctuated by the sporadic hiss of steam from the espresso machine. It was a hive of social and solo working, dotted around were lots of people speaking into their phones, or typing into their tablets as they sipped Salvo's coffee.

Arnie filed past them, they must be traders and operations managers. He found Jim sitting with Bob and Salvo at the far end by a window.

"Hey Arnie," said Bob, "you tasted Salvo's risotto yet? Best work food in the business."

"No, but I've heard all about it."

"Just you wait and see," beamed Salvo. He was smiling again.

"Right," said Slade as Arnie sat down, "the long and the short of it is that life is a little more complicated than it was on Monday eh? As well as Granwick for supplies, Muscorva for security, and Burridge and Perkins for accounts, we now have the Exemplary People1st Services Agency handling the HR for all our people around the world."

"I'm getting a headache," said Bob.

"As well you might," said Slade as a spring shower began spitting droplets of rain through a broken window frame at the next table a few feet from them. "But there's been another development…"

"I need to take a look at that window," interrupted Bob.

"You do that in a moment Bob. But don't fix it."

"Don't fix it?"

"That's right."

"Why not, there's water coming in?"

"That's exactly what I was about to tell you. From today

we work on internal markets. So you must price it first, then I have to authorise the cost, then you can do it."

"Internal market?"

"New working method for everyone. Put simply, we'll all have to price every job now and charge each other. Take this." Slade handed Bob a document.

"What is it?"

"It's the spec for the work for that window."

"The spec?"

"It outlines exactly what the job requires."

"I can see from here what the job requires."

"Yes but now it needs writing down."

"Why?"

"If we have an internal market all the exact requirements of the work need specifying bit by bit so we can judge the price. The clue's in the name; the spec."

"Right, so basically now we both assess the same job. How's that more efficient?"

"Well I suppose so. But it's called the contractor, client split."

"It's called bollocks. I've fixed hundreds of windows in this place over the years."

"Look Bob, I've had to adapt too, it took me all this morning to write the specs."

"You spent all morning writing out how to fix something that I already know how to fix?"

"You'll soon get the hang of it. It's all perfectly simple. I write out a spec for every job, you give me a price, and if you have met the spec I pay you from my budget into your budget. Got that, g..."

"No."

"Why not?"

"Can't I just fix the bloody thing before we get drenched?"

"No."

"Right so basically I read this and give you a price?"

"See it's simple. But be careful, I reckon I'll soon have to check if everything could be done by outside people cheaper. I can see that coming."

"Hey," said a trader with heavily gelled hair who was getting wet at his window seat, "can't you get this bloody window fixed!"

"I really should be doing the food order for Saturday's convention," said Salvo.

"Salvo stay there. This applies to you too. Maggie will be paying you from her budget into your budget, so you must cost it and give her the bill."

"Can't you just sign it off like always as my line manager?"

"Not from today. You must first get the costs from Granwick for the food..."

"Who do they get the food from?"

"They have their own list of approved food suppliers."

"... and I pass on the cost of that food to Maggie?"

"Almost."

"What then?"

"On top of that calculate your staff costs, overheads, wear and tear, kitchen operational costs, admin, plus of course your contingency, sundry services, oh and other on-costs for the day..."

"And?"

"...and then add all that onto the food bill. That's the total you then give to Maggie."

"Blimey."

"Then Maggie pays the whole lot from her budget to my budget?" asked Salvo.

"That's it. Then you pay Granwick for the food part of it... and they pay their approved food suppliers. Got that, good."

"Run that by me again," said Salvo.

"What a load of absolute total bollocks," said Bob.

Slade squinted at his laptop. "No Bob, it's hang on... 'increased budgetary responsibility through robust internal markets and streamlined outsourcing' ... well that's what it says here anyway."

"Will that make his risotto taste any better?" said Bob.

"How will I ever have time to cook it?" asked Salvo.

"You won't anymore. Welcome to new management Salvo," said Slade.

"So this crap will make the food worse."

"Possibly Bob."

"I'm hungry," shouted the hair gelled trader who was soaking wet and was now queuing at the counter. "Any chance of some bloody service here?"

"I'm too busy working to serve food," said Salvo.

"Unbelievable," said Bob.

"I hear you Bob," Slade's head slumped just a little.

Arnie looked around. The rain had increased slightly and several of the working traders and operations managers nearer the broken window had picked up their laptops and coffees and moved to drier tables. He glanced at his watch, anxiety rumbling through his belly, he needed to get back to Chartwell desperately. But he also needed Jim's help to get his Granwick account set up or he wouldn't get very far. Damn!

At that the heavens opened into a huge downpour, rain pouring in through the broken frame. Half of the canteen was now empty with gathering puddles, while the rest of the working guys were huddled into the dry spots around a few tables.

"Right Arnie same applies to you," said Slade above the noise of the rain pinging off the other windowpanes as the commotion of people moving settled down. "You will need to let me know how much each of your jobs is costing."

"So where do I...?"

"You get the prices for materials for each job from the catalogue on your Granwick account."

"But Jim I don't have a Granwick acc..."

"...Now then all of you," interrupted Slade. He bent down and picked up some folders from his case and handed one to each of them. "By the end of the week you will all need to read your service level agreements, which in simple language is the service you expect from each other."

"What the...?" Bob's mouth fell open.

Slade bent down and pulled out a pile of more files.

"What's this?" asked Arnie.

"Budget forms and costing sheets so that you can invoice each other for each job." Slade bent down again and emerged with some different files.

"What the hell...?" Salvo began.

"Audit guidelines. As you are budget holders now you will each have to sign that you've read them."

Slade disappeared again and came up with a handful of more folders.

"Now what...?" asked Bob.

"Your completed staff appraisal forms with my notes added. You all need to schedule to meet with me for an hour to see how you each feed this into your new personal performance targets. Got that, good."

The three took their appraisals. Slade reached down and pulled out a further wad of documents from a clipboard.

"And Bob, you take these..." He handed the huge pile across.

"What the fuck is all this?" asked Bob.

"The other specs for your jobs today. They took me all the early hours to write them. So after you've finished costing here, walk around the building and price these all up."

"You gotta be......"

"And don't mend anything."

The cook, the janitor, and the technician each went and sat at separate vacant tables, the driest ones they could each find that with the help of some kitchen roll and napkins could be made useable. The hard slashing of the rain eased after a few moments and the sun came out, throwing spring sunlight into the canteen that glinted off the floor puddles. They each got out their phones, a pen, and a notepad and started calculating.

An hour later the three were still deeply engrossed in their number crunching when a tall balding man in his fifties approached. A few of the traders had left their seats, closed their laptops, and walked out of the canteen as the rain had restarted.

"Ah Mr Friedman. We're enacting your instructions for Albion's new internal market," said Slade.

"Excellent. Modernisation and world beating performance is what we want."

"Er quite so. As you can see, they've all stopped work to calculate costs."

"Splendid!"

"It is all rather time consuming Mr Friedman," said Slade.

"It's total bollocks," came a voice from across the room.

"Increased efficiency Mr Slade. Why's that window letting in rain?"

"Because I'm too busy working out how much it will cost to actually go over and fix the bloody thing," said Bob.

"I see, I see," said Freidman, not looking at Bob. He squinted down to read the chef's name tag. "Now then, Mr Salvo is it, if I were you I'd fine Bob."

"Bollocks he will!"

"Hit him with an appropriate penalty charge Mr Salvo," continued Friedman.

"Salvo is my first name."

"If Maintenance Department are costing you trade because a repair goes over the set time in the agreement, well it really is your duty to instigate a penalty clause against his failure," he motioned towards Bob.

"Now hang on," said Bob.

"Well it is affecting my custom Bob," said Salvo.

"So I'll fix it."

"Sorry Bob, you can't till I have agreed a price," said Slade.

"That's the spirit Mr Slade!" said Friedman. "Excellent budgetary responsibility."

Slade glanced at his phone. "Damn I've just got an urgent message from Granwick. Looks like I've got to dash over there, another mix up with them and Burridge and Perkins regarding a shipment."

"And what's more this is fascinating," added Friedman after Slade had left, "because as far as I can see it's not the broken window that's causing all the problems, as the rain is only directly coming in on some of the tables. But for the other tables it's more the build-up of the puddles that's putting those parts of the canteen out of action."

"So?" asked Salvo.

"Well this is the wonder and the beauty of it..." said Friedman. "As Chief Budgetary Manager for Catering you can..."

"I thought I was Chief Cook...!"

"...you can either hit both janitor and Maintenance Department with separate penalty fines for their share of the neglect, or you can hit Bob with the entire penalty fine."

"Why's all this crap my fault!" said Bob.

"Then after Bob's budget has coughed up he can claim some of it back from the janitor for not mopping up the other puddles in time. On the spot market responsibility you see."

"So you want me to classify the different types of puddle...!"

"What did I do wrong?" asked Arnie.

Friedman ignored them. "It's up to you Mr Salvo. Devolved budgetary authority in action. On the spot empowerment. Wonderful gentlemen, keep up the good work. This is indeed progress," added Friedman as he left.

Bob looked at Salvo. "You're not hitting my bloody budget 'cos of that pissing window."

"Well my budget is hit with all these tables out of use," said Salvo suddenly moving to avoid getting hit with more droplets of rain.

"What bollocks. It's not like it's your money, you didn't even have a budget until ten minutes ago, so I dunno why you're getting so fussed about it. You were a bloody cook!"

"I'll clean it up," said Arnie, "well as soon as I can find a new mop."

"This is double bollocks," said Bob.

"It's double bollocks that you won't fix my window."

"Are you deaf I can't fix it, I'm not allowed to fix it yet!"

"Well why does it take so long to price up a simple fucking job like that!"

"For the same reason you won't fucking cook anything today and we're all bloody starving!"

"Well it's my canteen that you've fouled up, so you've got a fat penalty charge coming."

"Triple bollocks."

"And in future I'm not wasting my budget on you if any of my kitchen needs repairing. You're off my list. You're cancelled!"

"No, you're cancelled! Who wants to fix anything here anyway? I can choose who I sell my services to as from now. And fuck your risotto."

* * *

Arnie stood on the raised grassy bank as he left for home that night. The chances of getting the Chartwell ready ahead of time were gone, despite Bob having stayed behind a while to muck in.

It was good of Bob.

And even the chances of doing it on time were now getting tight.

He pinched the bridge of his nose, he had a sickly stress headache and the thought of messing up before Saturday now filled him with dread. He had only got back to Chartwell in the late afternoon again today. How could he realistically still be employed next week if he failed? Who would listen to excuses that would essentially amount to him criticising senior management?

Some chance.

It was late and the spring daylight was fading fast tonight. Arnie got out his phone and brought up Lucy's number. His fingers tapped out the message and his finger hovered over send... and hovered. He popped the phone back in his pocket, perhaps let it be again today.

He sat down on the banked grass, he had exhausted all his energy and verve before he could get started today. Damn, on top of everything he had forgotten to arrange his one-to-one appraisal wotsit with Jim. How on earth had Albion Bay grown so big and lasted so long if all the people that made it happen since 1855 were this sapped of spirit before they started each day. How often did those old pioneers have to fill out forms and audit their pickaxes? Only one thing for it, he would pop to the pub for a few to unwind.

He looked over at the Headquarters of the Greater Albion Bay Company where floors 4-9 shone so brightly they illuminated half the lawn.

But below that Floors 1, 2 and 3 were in darkness.

Friedman smiled and opened a report. "I am pleased to announce that our new internal market is a resounding triumph. I have seen for myself how devolved budgets are removing barriers and encouraging greater efficiency and financial responsibility. There is of course some early resistance, but it is clear to me that our modernisation is unleashing a new entrepreneurial spirit amongst the staff..."

"Absolutely," added Yates.

"The outsourcing programme is also progressing beyond all expectations. Human Resources has now been added to Accounts, Security, and Supplies. The Exemplary People1st Services Agency have also taken over our new payroll system, a valuable addition to our family of outside partners." Friedman stopped in case the man at the head of the table wanted to speak.

Devoux nodded for him to continue.

"The global contracting out of engineering, extraction, surveying, transport, and logistics on all our overseas sites is now well underway. The final redundancy bill is before you, and I am pleased to say it is less than initial estimates as some staff transferred to the new operators."

"Go on," said Devoux.

"But we have to push on, some of the staff are not up to the internal market yet, still too focused on getting jobs done."

"Modernisation would always test them," said Yates, "it's a work culture thing. Having some change deniers was inevitable."

"It's not too late to undo this," said Greta.

"We need to modernise, Mrs Rutherford."

"Not at the expense of so severely disrupting working arrangements, Mr Friedman."

"Staff will learn to adapt. Once the concept is embedded, once we have full buy-in, staff will automatically up their game to

avoid receiving penalty fines, and to win contracts off each other. It will become instinctive, second nature."

"And how much time and energy will that take out of each day?"

"Change always disrupts Mrs Rutherford, but it has to be done."

Greta sighed loudly. "Mr Friedman, we are in profit and our forecasts are already very good. But these forecasts will no doubt be dented by all these inward disruptions. Only yesterday we had to shelve Project Brunel because we are now so fragmented..."

Friedman cut in. "And to add further edge to staff performance, from tomorrow we will be setting robust daily output targets..."

"So Mr Friedman," Greta sighed again, "we'll have departmental targets, plus targets we want managers to set for staff in their appraisals, and now these daily output targets too?"

"Can't have too many targets, Mrs Rutherford."

"If I may," interrupted Yates taking off his large glasses. "I have a solution to all this."

"Go on," said Devoux.

"The release tomorrow of our new IT system. AlbionForward."

Friedman gave Yates a forced grin.

"Our existing IT system is absolutely fine," said Greta, "completely updated two years ago."

"This will empower managers to the next level," replied Yates, "instant situational updates."

"Our managers have always had instant situational updates. They each put in some frontline hours," said Greta. "There is no better situational update for management than that."

Yates sat upright and beamed. "Our new AlbionForward is designed for the needs of a modernised company, it will immediately eliminate any upgrading teething issues. The data capture will give us info at our fingertips as to how managers are working. It will cut costs and save time. From now on staff will be able to manage everything through AlbionForward; payments, budgets, internal markets, monitor their new targets, do their ordering, liaise with external suppliers, and record progress on every task. Staff will be empowered at a stroke with complete control at their fingertips, and shared information on hand instantly with a few clicks. And no more paper. The launch is tomorrow morning for all staff. We have set a target that from tomorrow afternoon everything shall be recorded through this system."

Devoux stared through narrow eyes. "Well in that case Mr Yates, you are responsible for meeting that target."

FRIDAY

Arnie stamped the button to fire up the heavy duty cleaner he had nicknamed 'Tyson' and attacked the renovators' dust with gusto.

Only one day to go. But at last he was working!

It had taken ages yesterday to look up the prices of everything in the Granwick catalogue and fill out the new forms, but at least he had finally got his account set up and placed his order. But all hopes of Arnie sampling that risotto an enthusiastic chef had promised yesterday were in vain. He wouldn't have had time to eat it anyway. But this morning was already different.

He was winning!

Arnie whistled as he steered the hungry Tyson about. And there was more progress too, hopefully he at last had some spare company overalls coming as part of the new order. And a new mop. He hit the button and Tyson fell silent. Right, he would give the toilet floors a good going over with the scrubbing machine and leave them to be drying while he vacuumed the carpet in the main Chartwell Suite.

He was buzzing!

He glanced at the brass work, it could do with a final seeing to. But he would still be short of stuff until his order arrived. He was still wondering what to do about that when Bob and another technician appeared, a blonde woman with a bob cut and Alison written on her name badge. Arnie nodded a greeting toward her.

"Good to meet you Arnie, hope you're settling in okay," Alison said in a strong Irish accent.

"Ah yes I've seen your desk, same to you Alison."

"Ach, its Ali, except to me mother or when I'm in church. Oh and me rugby coach, he's a bit of a bloody stickler too."

Arnie chuckled. "Listen Bob, I couldn't borrow some detergent could I? Just for a few hours, I have my order coming this morning."

"Hey man yesterday of course I would have, but we're all about internal markets now. It's no longer all for one and one for all, it's every man for himself."

"And woman," smiled Alison.

"Oh right, yeah I suppose so."

"Tell you what though," said Bob rubbing his chin, "you've got some lubricant on your trolley haven't you?"

"Yeah, from the batch I bought the other day."

"Well I'm still waiting for mine, Granwick haven't delivered it yet. Hopeless."

"So?"

"Well, how about a trade, your lubricant for my bleach and detergent?"

"A trade?"

"Yeah a trade."

"I dunno, are we allowed?"

"Isn't that what they told us yesterday, that what we do

now is charge each other? Internal markets and all that crap."

"I suppose."

"So I'll pay you for the lubricant with my cleaning stuff?"

"OK, deal," said Arnie as they shook hands and exchanged their stuff.

"What in the name of God is going on here?" asked Ali. "I was only off a few days." She turned and helped Bob heave a huge speaker onto a stand. "Now aren't we a team and a half," she beamed as she high fived Bob.

Arnie pivoted away to get back to work.

"Hey Arnie," Bob called him back. "Just between you and me..."

"What...?"

Bob leaned in. "Sorry mate, but I can see this place is scrubbing up and all that, even from when I left here yesterday. But you know...well with just a day to go..."

"...Bob, I know it. I just seem to be busting a gut all the time and getting nowhere."

"Tell me about it. Last week me and Ali would have dropped everything, got stuck in with you all day, whatever."

Ali nodded. "No two ways about it Arnie."

"But now we can't mate, Friedman's new daily output targets. We've booked in loads of smaller things so that we can meet the number of jobs we have to finish today. We had to leave the bigger ones, the things that really need doing, like say the top floor air con before it goes totally haywire. But there's no way we'd meet his daily quota if we took that on. Half a day at least, if not more."

"Jeez, it seems that common sense has gone out the window altogether," Ali added.

"It's total bollocks, but what else can we do?"

Arnie sighed. "I suppose it's progress, what do the likes of us know."

He stamped on the start button of the vacuum cleaner and grabbed the hose. Time to get back to it...

His phone went, it was Slade. Arnie silenced the vacuum cleaner and put him on speakerphone.

"Arnie where are you?"

"Chartwell."

"Is Bob up there with you?"

"Yeah I'm here with Ali doing the sound system."

"You all need to stop work."

"What!"

"Get yourselves down to the Pioneers Room. It's the launch of our new online intranet, Mr Yates himself has said all staff must be present. Bob, record how many minutes you spent so far on that job so you and Ali can pick up where you left off. We need to price the time so you charge Maggie's budget the right amount. The launch starts in 10 minutes."

Arnie put a hand to his forehead.

Shit!

* * *

The Pioneers Room was already packed, all the seats filled, with many others standing around the edges. Arnie stood with the crowd at the back beside Bob, Ali, and Slade. Ahead he could see some of the traders that he recognised, sitting with their arms folded, sighing heavily. Some were staring at their watches and fidgeting.

"How long will this take?" asked Arnie.

"I've no idea," answered Slade, "it's up to Mr Yates."

At that Yates, bedecked in a dark T-shirt with 'AlbionForward' emblazoned across it, took to the floor. Holding the microphone he asked some of the Albion IT Team at the front to stand up along with some strangers in suits.

"I am delighted to welcome our representatives from the Forever Forward IT Solutions Company who partnered us in designing this site. Working with the digital engagement team and other stakeholders, the new system is designed to sit alongside existing principles of design and structure to enable a revised staff-facing global information architecture that provides a level of consistency and functionality that will reduce both mainte-nance costs and technical debt as any future changes to staff interface can be deployed from a central code base. Now then..."

"What in the name of God is he talking about?" whispered Ali.

"I've no bloody idea," replied Bob. "Just another Work Prevention Officer trying to look good and justify their job. And I bet there's a few million shillings an hour sitting in front of us thinking the same thing."

"....and as a result we have also adopted 'Forward' into our IT name to signify our never ending striving for improvement. So the new internal website of the Greater Albion Bay Company will henceforth be known as AlbionForward. AlbionForward is a bespoke innovative robust and agile solution focused on indi-vidual accountability through a collective portal ..."

"Ah now," whispered Ali, "to be fair he does look rather pleased with himself."

Arnie shuffled his feet and checked his watch.

* * *

After the speeches, the presentation, the Q and A session, the introductions to the IT company team, and the guided talk through the AlbionForward familiarisation handouts -

all available on pdf with video support on YouTube, Arnie hurried out.

He had got a text that his order had arrived downstairs. At last! With that collected, he would get straight back to Chartwell and to work. He may have lost the morning but this afternoon he would be flying.

Ain't no stopping me now!

Downstairs Arnie approached one of the security team.

"I've got a package to collect."

"Don't know nothing about it mate."

"Well, it was delivered here."

"I've just come on, I only work for Muscorva casual. How do you expect me to know?"

Arnie tried the outhouse with the spider tattoo on his huge neck, but he held up a dismissive hand to instruct Arnie not to bother him while he sorted something on his phone. Arnie approached a third bruiser.

"You need to speak to Head of Security, Maz."

"Well where is he?"

"Dunno."

"Well who do I ask?"

"Dunno. He might be outside innit."

Outside, Arnie found a lean muscley guy with Maz on his badge having a cigarette.

"Did a package arrive for me earlier, for Arnold Smeggins?"

"Yeah," Maz said stubbing out. "Come inside with me."

Arnie followed him inside to a corner of the downstairs lobby where he was handed a big open cardboard box. On the top were sets of overalls in cellophane under which was the cleaning stuff he needed.

"And the mop?" Arnie asked.

"What?"

"Me mop. Where's me mop?"

"Dunno nothing about it mate. That's all they dropped off. Here, check the doc that's signed."

Arnie gazed at it, there was indeed no mention of a mop. *What the hell did this provisions company have against mops.* Right later he would go out and buy his own bloody mop. But at least for now he could get into some overalls that weren't torn.

He nipped into the toilet on the ground floor, opened the cellophane and donned the first pair. In the mirror he looked ridiculous, they were at least two sizes too big. Damn!

He removed the other set from the cellophane. The company crest on his breast pocket was mis-spelt '*Albino*'.

Putting these on was a struggle to get his legs in, then a battle to pull them over his midriff. He breathed in, squeezed his belly, and tugged. Once he had won the battle to get them on he checked himself in the mirror, his little pot belly was bursting a button. Well he couldn't walk around with his knee out forever, and the bigger pair were not safe to work in with all that loose clothing flopping about. He'd have to make the best of these tight ones for now. They must be at least two sizes too small. Something else to sort out next week.

Arnie grabbed the cleaning box and headed for the lift. He found that if he waddled with his feet splayed at 'five to one' the overalls pinched a little less.

He arrived at Chartwell and rubbed his hands; time to get stuck in. Now where was he up to, oh yeah the carpet in the main Suite... then back to Tyson.

Only a day to go.

He could do this.

Yes he could.

And as he spoke to himself his spirits lifted. Arnie felt a smile spread across his face. He switched on the vacuum cleaner and grabbed the tube to start. Right let's go.

His phone went.

"Arnie where are you?"

"Just got back to Chartwell Jim."

"Mr Yates wants everybody to set up their personal AlbionForward account immediately."

"Immediately?"

"That's right. He says AlbionForward must be live for all staff by this afternoon. So come to the canteen, I reckon the quickest way to get this sorted is if you all work together. Got that, good."

Arnie switched off the vacuum cleaner.

Oh for fuck's sake!

* * *

On fourth, Arnie readied himself for the hiss of the espresso machine, the smell of mocha and the hum of lively work chatter.

The lift opened to silence and a stale smell of bad coffee. *What!*

He waddled through where Salvo's canteen had been yesterday, where now half a dozen vending machines were dispensing foul smelling drinks into paper cups. Another machine was dropping out some sweating prepacked sand-wiches and chocolate bars.

The small café style tables had gone, now there were just a few tumbler chairs about with mini tables and in each corner bins overflowed with used paper cups and sandwich wrappers. Only a handful of traders were here.

"Blimey Arnie, have you put on weight?" asked Bob.

"And would ya mind telling us who the hell are the Albino Company?" Ali laughed.

"Very funny both of you." Arnie glanced around. "Am I on the right floor?"

"I'm afraid so," Slade answered. "Catering has been outsourced. Salvo and his team have been made redundant along with their fresh food. From now on your food and drink will be from these machines. All serviced by the Ovlas Catering Company, via Granwick of course."

"Oh of course," smirked Bob.

"And take these," Slade handed out some leaflets.

"What's this?" asked Ali.

"Albion's new healthy eating guides to replace the fresh food."

Ali winced.

"Right then," Slade said as he pulled some small laptops out of a case, "let's get this done so we can all get on with our day. What they didn't clarify in that two hour session was the gist of AlbionForward."

"I'm all ears," said Bob.

"So basically, one click is all you need."

"And to do what in God's name?" asked Ali.

"So you just sign in here..."

"And..." asked Bob.

"...and once signed in you can order supplies, check your roster, recharge each other, deal with outside suppliers, check the time allowed for each job. Plus from noon today the new rule is that we record everything we do here, so you must now update your progress after every task. Got that, goo..."

"Not really, sorry," said Arnie.

"So for example Arnie, click on the Supply tab here and

it takes you straight to Granwick for any issues you have with them."

"Oh right," said Arnie thinking of his mop and overalls.

"...or click on 'Accounts' here, to transfer money and it will link to Burridge and Perkins ..."

"A bit like walking to Floor 2 to see Sue, or Floor 3 to see Sandeep," said Bob.

"So," added Slade, "there's a few laptops about so you need to each set up your own AlbionForward account. It takes about half an hour. You'll need your phone as they'll text you a code. Mr Yates wants this done right away so the whole company is up and running on it."

"Just as well we have nothing else to do," said Bob, "we do have a sound system to set up."

"Right I have to leave you folks to it," said Slade getting up, "I've been pinged. Looks like I have an urgent conference call with Granwick to follow up on yesterday's confusion. I reckon I could be tied up a while. And by the way I wouldn't go for the coffee if I were you, well not from that end machine anyway," he said tipping away a full cup of brown liquid.

* * *

An hour later Bob, Arnie and Ali were still sat around their laptops trying to set up their AlbionForward accounts in what used to be Salvo's canteen. Bob was swearing at the screen, while Arnie had just popped into the Gents to revert to his torn overalls, the tight pair had started to hurt.

"Right where you up to?" asked Bob.

"I'm on the 'Staff Details' page," answered Ali.

"Me too," said Arnie as he returned.

"Nice knee mate," said Bob.

"Is that designer?" grinned Ali.

"Very funny."

There was a moment's silence as they each tapped in to confirm the data the site had on them.

"Ah it wants payroll number," said Bob, "I think I've got my last payslip."

Arnie reached into his pocket, glanced sideways at the papers Sandeep had given him, and rapidly slipped them back into his pocket, pushing them down as deep as they would go.

"Right, department number," added Bob. "I never even knew we had department numbers."

"We probably didn't up to now," said Ali. "It says if unsure get that from your HR Department."

"How can we. There is no HR Department anymore!"

"Well don't be having a go at me, that's what it says. I guess we have to get it from Exemplary People whatever they're called?" replied Ali.

"How?" asked Arnie sneaking a glance at his watch.

"Didn't Jim say we contact them through AlbionForward on here somehow," replied Ali.

"How the hell can we do that, we don't have this account set up yet," said Bob.

"Well I don't know, is there a helpline or something?" Ali scanned the screen.

"Yes there's a number at the bottom here," said Arnie.

Bob dialled the number and placed his phone on speakerphone...

'*Welcome to the Exemplary People1st Services Agency, your call is important to us. These calls may be recorded for training purposes and to help with our constant strive for improvement. We believe that people matter, and that is our business. So that we may help you as quickly as possible, please state your company name after the beep.'*

"Albion Bay," said Bob into the mouthpiece.

I'm sorry I didn't catch that.

"Albion Bay," Bob repeated into the phone.

Did you say Eleanor Gay?

"No."

I'm sorry I didn't catch that.

"NO!"

Thank you. Please repeat your company name.

"ALBION BAY," Bob said loudly.

I'm sorry I didn't catch that.

"A_L_B_I_O_N B_A_Y."

Did you say Albion Bay?

"Yes."

I'm sorry I didn't catch that.

"Oh for fuck's sake. Yes!"

I'm sorry I didn't catch that.

"YES!!!"

Thank you. Now please enter your four digit department code and username.

"How the fuck can I do that. That's what I'm trying to set up!"

I'm sorry I didn't catch that.

"Oh go screw yourself!"

I'm sorry I didn't catch that.

"Oh fuck off…"

"You're talking to a machine Bob," laughed Ali.

"Oh yeah," Bob gave a frustrated chuckle as he hung up. "This is total crap. And it's knackering, I'd much rather be working."

So would I, thought Arnie. He glanced at his watch again, how was he ever going to get back to Chartwell.

"I'll have to call IT," said Ali.

Twenty minutes later an Albion IT guy wearing a faded Fleetwood Mac T shirt and blue rimmed glasses arrived. "Having a bit of trouble are we. Not read the guidance pdf properly I suppose. Dear, dear."

Bob gave him a glare as Ali explained the problem.

The IT guy rolled his eyes. "It's perfectly simple. If you haven't registered, just enter your staff payroll number and the six digit user code that is valid for five minutes that is sent to the app on your phone which will then generate your four digit unique departmental pin code which you then enter to set up your memorable place, date, username, and password to enable you to register. However if you have already registered, simply enter your new username and new departmental pin code to generate the random six digit code on your app and then insert that to bring up the sign in page where you can then..."

"Eh...?"

An hour later Ali's, Arnie's, and Bob's AlbionForward accounts had been set up by the IT guy who had announced that his preferred name was Fleetwood.

"Great," said Arnie, "I'm off back to Chartwell." He got up and hurried towards the lifts.

"Hang on," said Fleetwood.

Arnie stopped near the door to the lobby.

"I take it you now have access to your internal email accounts?"

"Yep I have mine," said Ali.

"Blimey," said Bob, "I already have over 140 bloody emails!"

"Well I suggest you get to reading them," said Fleetwood. "And don't forget to answer ones that are invites to the virtual staff café for the wider Albion family. Our online meeting place that shows how much the company cares."

"I hope it serves better coffee than this one," said Ali.

"And done the training have we?"

"What training?" the three asked in unison.

"Tut, tut. Read your emails. Now that you have access to our new IT system you all need to immediately complete your Data and Information Protection online training course."

"Immediately!" Arnie started walking back to the others.

"Immediately on gaining access. It's a requirement. How many more times, read your new emails. It's got a multiple choice test at the end, so best take notes as you work through it. If you fail you will be excluded from other parts of the site, but you do get the chance to do it again straight away."

"How long will this take," Arnie's voice was shrill as he sat back down in his same seat.

"It takes as long as it takes. And don't forget to hit 'submit' so the company records show that you've done it. And don't forget as well to sign the form at the end. Electronic signature of course.

"You are joking?" said Ali.

"You will get a certificate for doing it."

Bob pulled a face.

"And you all need to pay from your budgets into my budget for the time I just spent here."

"Jeez, this is like working in a different world altogether," said Ali.

Fleetwood started handing out some papers. "Here's the feedback forms asking what you think of AlbionForward. If you wish to give ten out of ten for each question, that's fine and I will take your responses now. But if on any questions you wish to give less than top marks, please take the time to stay behind later after work to explain why in detail. That's because your voice matters, and we want to hear how to improve from you people on the frontline."

"Yeah right," said Bob, "as if what we put will matter with this new lot. Ron used to talk about this crap, but he did it as a joke."

Bob and Ali quickly ticked ten out of ten all the way down and bunged their forms straight back to Fleetwood. Arnie watched and quickly did the same. He needed to muster every second he could spare this evening dealing with Chartwell.

"Good," Fleetwood said collecting the papers, "and don't forget to complete the other online courses."

"What other online courses?"

"On next generation risk assessments, managing change, budgeting, latest display screen regulations, the internal customer, the green workspace, safeguarding, assertiveness, diversity, teamworking, empowerment, inclusivity, and well-being at work. Read your emails. But you have a week to do those. And don't forget to sign that you've read everything."

"Blimey, somebody up there is desperate to cover their own arse," said Ali.

"All the online courses are the same format," continued Fleetwood, "that's the beauty of our new AlbionForward. Clever eh? And you must all update your staff profiles immediately too before the system will work, you can customise them if you like. Think of a nice, preferred work name if you want. Like I did."

"All this and I can't get a mop?"

* * *

In the middle of the afternoon Slade arrived back. "How's it going?"

"We've just finished the online course this minute," answered Arnie.

Bob pulled a face. "I can't wait to frame my certificate."

"It took that long?" asked Slade.

"Before we could start we all had to create our new staff profiles which took forever," said Ali, "and then the questions were so badly written and confusing. On some of them any of the answers could have been right."

"Nice pictures though," smirked Bob.

"Sure, hasn't being glossy always been a grand way to cover that you don't know what you're doing," added Ali.

"And exactly how is this place any more secure now after us doing all this bloody crap than it was this morning?" said Bob. "We didn't learn a thing."

"Ah now," Ali grinned, "don't forget that apart from some arses being covered upstairs, we've also helped justify other people's existence in backrooms. Crucial is that. Then we've also made senior management feel like they're doing something. All very important. Sure it's what we're here for."

"Yeah, more like to keep our Work Prevention Teams upstairs in a job. Total bollocks."

"Well it's all done now. Good," said Slade. "Now Arnie, without Ron's team, Granwick will be sending a firm to deliver the convention furniture sometime today or tomorrow morning; you know a few hundred chairs, tables, stands and so on. So best plan for that disruption with all that arriving..."

Shit! More obstacles!

"And I'll need to schedule you all in for the new staff appraisal meetings with me based on the forms you filled in. Each one will take about an hour or so."

Double shit!

"And you will each need to meet individually with an auditor now you hold budgets. Schedule your own meeting with them through Burridge and Perkins."

Triple shit!

Bob stood up. "Right then, I'll be off now folks."

Slade looked at him quizzically.

"My early finish Jim. Remember, I took time off in lieu instead of overtime for staying behind to help on Monday?"

"Oh yes of course, sorry Bob. I've been a bit distracted lately. Take a seat for a second will ya while I put this through AlbionForward so you can get away." Slade tapped keys and talked aloud to himself. "Right now, I sign in here, open the portal there, go to staffing here, linking to Exemplary People whatever they're called there…"

Jim Slade went quiet.

"What is it?" asked Bob.

"Uhm …well there's annual leave, compassionate leave, parental leave, sickness …and so on… and over here there's a separate thing for overtime."

"But…?"

"Well, there doesn't seem to be anywhere to record time off in lieu. Weird. Hang on I'll call Mr Yates."

Slade took his phone and walked across the repository of plastic smells, paper cups and overflowing bins that used to be Salvo's buzzing canteen. From where he was sitting Arnie could hear Slade's agitated voice.

Slade came back, thunder on his brow. "I'm sorry Bob but I'm afraid you won't be able to go early."

"Why not?"

"Because AlbionForward doesn't recognise time off in lieu."

"But the firm does! Standard practice for years."

"True. But Mr Yates says we must now be governed only by what this website will let us do."

"What!"

"Everything has to go through the system."

"I thought the other day they said they wanted more flexibility, responsibility, and initiative?"

"Well yes, but only via this system though Bob."

"But we've arranged the little one's birthday now. She's expecting me in half an hour. We agreed it."

Arnie looked at Slade, his body was slouched and there was pain across his face.

"I know Bob, I get it, and it was good of you to muck in," replied Slade. "But my hands are tied. On Monday we were working in a different world. I'll sign the overtime for you now Bob if you like. I can do that because there's a box for it."

"But Jim, I helped save a deal…"

"I know you did. Look, I spoke to Mr Yates and explained everything. He said thank you for the feedback and they will add 'time off in lieu' to the AlbionForward site at the next IT review or whatever. He says your voice matters."

"So why isn't time off in lieu on there in the first place?"

"Apparently they didn't really understand it as a standard work practice."

"And I suppose they didn't think to ask anyone first? What bollocks."

"But for now Bob the message that Mr Yates asked me to relay to you was, 'if his official rostered time on AlbionForward is 5 o'clock, he should work until then. His time is his time'. His words I'm afraid."

"What!"

"That's the message, I'm sorry Bob. Look I've been called out to Burridge and Perkins, something's gone wrong over there, I have to go." Slade left, his shoulders rounded, his gait different, kicking some paper cups that littered the floor as he left.

Bob slouched in his chair, a look of injustice branded across his brow. Ali put her arm around him and gave him a hug.

"Total bollocks," muttered Bob. "At that briefing they said they're coming up with all this crap for us to use our initiative, and we're more in a straitjacket now than we've ever been."

"Want a coffee?" Ali joked.

Bob glared at her. "And when we do put ourselves out to save a company deal you get shat on. I mean what's all that crap from Yates that 'my time is my time' as if I'm trying to take the piss by skiving off. The fucking cheek of it. I mean, it was me that gave up my time in the first place. And I gave up more than I was gonna take back anyway. So by their system, from now on I'll be giving them less. That's brains upstairs for you that is, for fuck's sake. I tell ya, this is becoming a 'just do your time' and 'keep your head down' place. I won't be putting myself out for this place anymore."

With senior management out of the way the staff were able to get back to work.

Bob and Ali finished setting up the sound system, then spent just as long again logging onto AlbionForward to record they had completed the task. Arnie worked feverishly for the rest of the afternoon and then on into the evening to make up lost time. Maybe he should have protested about the distractions today, but how could he without admitting he was slipping, and without looking like he was asking to be a special case, everybody else was being distracted as well. And without criticising management too. That would not have been a good idea.

At 7.30 he was rubbing down the brass rails when he heard footsteps in the lobby. He gazed at the entrance to see who would appear.

"Hello," Arnie called out.

Nothing.

"Is anybody there?"

He walked through the suite and out into the empty lobby. The lift doors were just closing. Looking up at the little lights he clocked that the lift was going to ground floor. Odd.

He walked back into the main Chartwell Suite and resumed his work.

Don't think about what's left to do. Just keep cracking on. Keep cracking on...

* * *

Late that night Arnie dipped his hands into his pockets as he kicked a large stone up the pebbled path on his way home. His head was spinning. He left the path near its end, wandered onto the lawn and then up the little green bank. He pulled his phone out, then thrust it back without looking at it.

Chartwell wasn't ready and he was on the brink of exhaustion. He wasn't sure if he could do enough tomorrow morning to get it ready in time, he would grab a few hours' sleep, then get in early and try. Damn he'd forgotten to update his progress on that bloody AlbionForward website thingy. He would have to do that before he started tomorrow.

The original enthusiasm had morphed into a sickly stress feeling, but that had now given way to a hollow gut-wrenching disappointment at his failure. How had it all slipped?

It didn't make sense.

He looked back at the building from the raised grassy bank. In the fading evening daylight the lights of the Head-quarters of the Greater Albion Bay Company were still on from Floor 5 upwards, but the bottom 4 layers, like Arnie's mood, were dark.

BOARDROOM, FLOOR 9...

The champagne cork popped to a loud cheer, and the glasses overflowed.

Devoux raised his glass, "To a modernised Albion."

"To a modernised Albion," echoed Friedman and Yates as they stood and clinked glasses. Greta sat in silence touching her pearl necklace.

Devoux sat down and nodded to Yates. "Please begin."

Yates smiled at Devoux. "I am delighted to announce that the roll out of AlbionForward is an unqualified success. All staff are now live on the system with no disruption to working arrangements and we have live situational updates on every task. The staff feedback is extremely positive. An overwhelming 99% of responses gave maximum marks across all questions."

Friedman leaned forward. "Wonderful Mr Yates. And our internal markets are bedding in nicely with excellent staff buy-in. Plus the new robust daily output targets are adding real edge to staff performance. More jobs than ever getting done."

The air con made a loud screeching noise.

Yates waited for the din to ease. "Indeed Mr Friedman. And I am delighted to also report that the Exemplary People1st Services Agency are now operating our new state of the art payroll system and it's performing beyond all expectations."

Friedman leaned further forward. "Indeed Mr Yates. And as for the outsourcing, our external partners are bringing their expertise to the table. I would go as far as to say our managers are flourishing in their new environment."

Yates took off his glasses. "Indeed Mr Friedman. And the new performance indicators and staff appraisals are changing our work culture. We'll soon be asking managers to introduce other modernising influences like staff peer reviews, 360 degree assessments, and staff wellbeing audits."

The air con spluttered again a few more times before something started rattling.

Friedman waited for the noise to abate. "Excellent Mr Yates. And we have now sold about half of our overseas sites. For the locations we haven't sold, we have several parties interested in leasing them, which we prefer as it avoids the need for our oversight if we give them full operational responsibility. Negotiations are at an advanced stage, there's a full breakdown before you. AlbionForward will receive receipts from the leases automatically, reducing our need for a large pool of Finance staff."

Devoux smiled. "Go ahead with the leasing of the last of our overseas sites Mr Friedman."

"More music to my ears Mr Devoux."

The air con made a loud clicking noise.

"This makes us more vulnerable to circumstances, not less," said Greta.

Friedman beamed. "And the beauty of this, is that by selling most of the sites outright as a sweetener we can negotiate better lease deals for the ones we do keep, plus we get the instant capital in the short term from the sales."

"And in the long term?" asked Greta.

Devoux put down his champagne glass. "There is no such thing as the long term Mrs Rutherford. Only the next short term after this one."

SATURDAY

Game over.

Arnie switched off Tyson and waited as the beast whined down into silence. He had gotten in early this Saturday morning, but the hours of graft hadn't achieved as much as he had hoped. He heard Lucy, '*you just never get it right, do you, totally bloody useless.*'

But if he was useless, he was not dishonest. He would own up now. Arnie took a deep breath, right let's get this over with. They'd find out soon enough anyway and it was best coming from him.

He phoned Slade's office. Bob picked up the phone.

"Hi Bob, it's Arnie I was looking for Jim."

"Hey Arnie, Jim is down in the Pioneers Room."

"Oh right, thanks Bob."

"And Arnie..."

"...yeah I'm still here..."

"...Yates wants his staff wellbeing audits done."

"What staff wellbeing audits?"

"It's a new survey thingy for our welfare. All these daft questions are really stressing me out."

"How long do I have to do it?"

"A week max apparently. But it takes forever, I'm only just finishing mine."

"Oh right, thanks for the heads up. Catch you later Bob."

"Maybe, maybe not. My shift finishes at 12.30 today. Ali is on rota this afternoon to cover the convention. If not see you Monday."

Arnie called the lift. Damn he'd forgotten to update his progress on AlbionForward from yesterday, and now he hadn't entered this morning's progress too. He went back into Chartwell and switched on the tablet. He attempted to log in. An error message appeared; the AlbionForward system was down.

Shit, he'd probably be in more trouble for not updating his work records last night. And he hadn't booked to see an auditor yet, nor had his staff appraisal meeting. Now a bloody staff wellbeing audit to do as well. And all those other online courses.

Oh well, you can only get hung once.

He went back to the lobby and called the lift again. He had restless feet as he waited, pacing back and forth. He really should have told Jim earlier he was failing. That was obvious now. Somehow he had thought he could pull this off. He had made great progress at times, so it had been a reasonable thought. After all, the toilets and the lobby were now shining. And the carpet wasn't too bad, and the brass was coming along, and the builder's dust was gone.

Yep, he could have cracked all this in a few days if he had been left alone.

But that all said, by yesterday he should have owned up. One distraction too many. Perhaps he had got stuck in the groove that he would be able to graft his way through this.

Or was it that he had been too afraid to admit he was sinking?

It was hard to tell anymore.

He scratched his head and entered the lift, strange nobody had checked on him yet. And where was the delivery of the hundreds of extra chairs that were meant to be here? And the tables? And odd there was no catering company here yet either. Oh well that didn't matter now.

'Albion can rely on me.' His words made his stomach hollow. He exited the lift, passed the trophy cabinet at the Floor 5 lobby, and went through the door marked '*Operations Managers*'.

What!...

Ahead of him was a cavernous empty space, all the office furniture and the partitions had gone. A gloomy looking Slade was stomping out from the Pioneers Room ahead. He met Arnie halfway across the ocean of bare office grey carpet.

"Have all the operations managers gone?" asked Arnie, his voice echoing in the vast open area.

"Aye lad. Albion have laid off all the overseas staff. Other firms are going to be running most of our sites for us, and our other sites we're selling off. There's no need for operations managers if we won't operate anything anymore. That's what was announced anyway. We will probably have some extra rent collectors on our floor in the Traders' Room looking after the leases, so you might be busier there next week."

"Yeah ok I..."

"And by the way Arnie, AlbionForward crashed this morning."

"Yeah Jim I saw that," Arnie shuffled his feet. "Jim, I need to have a word with you please." His voice came out feeble, despite how hard he had tried to sound normal. "There's something I need to tell you."

"Sure Arnie, just hang on one moment will you."

"It's kind of urgent Jim. It's about the convention today, the Chartwell Suite isn't..."

"Sure, just give me a couple of minutes. You just caught me as I was heading downstairs. I've got something there to sort out first that's also urgent. Look, meet me down at the entrance in ten will ya. You can tell me then. Whatever it is, ten minutes I hope won't make a difference."

"I suppose not."

Ten minutes later Arnie arrived down in the lobby. Maggie and Jim were deep in conversation with a new security guy and a smartly dressed Asian woman with shoulder length hair and 'Hasna, Marketing' on her name tab. Bob was standing by.

"...I'm just saying nobody here knows anything about it," the new security guy said.

"What do you mean nobody knows anything about it?" said Slade. "We've sent countless emails to your company about deliveries all week. I even came down to brief your guy on the ground here, the one who was in charge here the other day, I think his name was Maz. He said it was fine."

"Maz is not here, I took over today."

"What do you mean Maz is not here?"

"Our firm are short staffed, so they sent him to work at the gig today."

"Gig?"

"The rock concert in the park. Our firm is doing the security for it, Maz was sent there to supervise."

"Not our problem," said Maggie. "We pay your firm to be here. Look, before I phone your office is there anything you can tell me that may be a semblance of use."

"I can only guess the furniture delivery was just sent away."

"But why on earth would someone do that?" asked Hasna.

"Nobody who is on today was told anything about it. Not our fault is it."

"What total bollocks," said Bob.

"This is a waste of time, we're going around in bloody circles." said Maggie. "Hasna, get onto the suppliers and see if we can get the seats and tables back. I'll deal with this security firm later, no time now."

"Right away," said Hasna.

Maggie turned back to the security guy, "Has the food arrived yet?"

"What food?"

"The caterers. For the convention."

"Dunno. Not that I've seen, and I've been here all morning."

"Damn they're late," said Maggie getting out her phone. "I'll call Granwick. She pressed the phone and held it to her ear. *My customer number? Oh to hell with that piffle. Listen this is the Greater Albion Bay Company and we pay you. So you find it. I want to speak to somebody in authority there immediately.*"

Arnie shuffled his feet and hesitated. Jim was alone at last, but things seemed to be getting tense, it might be best to hold a moment before confessing. A second later and the chance was lost, Jim was now on his phone too.

Eventually Maggie came back over. "Right Jim, the top and bottom of it is that Granwick are saying that Burridge and Perkins did not send the advance payment to the caterers, and Burridge and Perkins are saying that the order wasn't placed correctly by Granwick. It seems to have slipped between the two of them."

Hasna hung up her phone. "It seems the delivery for the furniture was sent away by Muscorva Security. They say they can still come back, but it might not be for an hour or two now."

"So we're still in with a faint chance of having some bloody furniture in time!"

"Not so sure," said Slade, also just hanging up. "Exemplary People1st were supposed to hire the casual staff to help set up, I'm trying to find where these troops are. Seems Granwick may not have processed the order. Right now Exemplary People1st are not answering the phone."

"If AlbionForward is back up maybe we can check on that?" asked Maggie.

"No it's still down," said Hasna.

"Well you'll just have to work your magic Jim."

"We don't have the in-house troops to be flexible anymore Maggie. All gone. I told Granwick it would be tight having all these logistics on the morning of the event. I'm not sure they've done events like this before."

"Great," said Maggie. "So even if we do get some bloody furniture we are not sure if we have enough people to set the whole thing up in time, and even if we did, we don't know if we have any bloody food. God it's all so fragmented. Disaster, complete bloody disaster. This could cost us big time. Lost goodwill, lost opportunities for renewals."

"It's not the Albion I know," said Slade.

"It's total bollocks."

"I mean look at us, phoning around bloody contractors like a bunch of amateurs just to do the simplest of things. Me and Hasna should be going through the sales pitches now with our team, not distracted with this rubbish. And why is nobody from the board here today, the Hudsons were always here for this..."

"Hi folks," said a vaguely familiar voice behind them.

They all turned to check.

"Salvo!"

"Yep it's me."

"What the hell you doing here?" asked Maggie.

"Have my dips ever let you down yet?"

"You mean...?"

"Oh come on. You mean none of you spotted that the 'Ovlas Catering Company' is Salvo backwards," he said his usual fixed smile now a beam. "Salvo Cordella, at your service."

"How long have you had that company?" asked Maggie.

"About ten minutes."

Slade laughed.

"When they made me redundant I set up the company straight away, I got on Granwick's approved list, and won the deal. I saw this coming, that's why I quizzed you about the approved list the other day Jim. I told them I knew the clientele and this market. That sort of rubbish. Turns out it wasn't rubbish though, as I knew the gig was on this Saturday I prepped for it in advance, despite the mix up with the orders and the paperwork."

"Good to have you back," said Maggie.

"Even better for me," Salvo beamed again. "I'm earning far more out of Albion as a contractor today than I ever did as staff. And the beauty of it is I'm doing less. Madness. But lovely madness. So where do I set up the food, up in Chartwell I suppose?"

Arnie's heart skipped.

"There seems to be a bit of a muddle," said Slade.

"Chartwell has no furniture, so it seems it can't be used for the convention."

"No matter to me nowadays," said Salvo with that same grin. "I'm a contractor so I'll still be paid."

"What total bollocks," said a voice behind Arnie.

Maggie took a loud deep breath. "Right I am not beaten yet," she said striding away.

There was a moment of silence.

"Right now," Slade placed his hand on Arnie's shoulder, "so what did you want to see me about that's so urgent?"

"Er nothing Jim."

"Are you sure?"

Arnie's stomach hollowed, a mixture of relief and guilt. But he needed to keep this job.

"Yep. All's fine Jim."

"Double sure?" Slade held his gaze, hand still on the shoulder.

Arnie nodded.

"Ok Arnie if you say so, that's fine." Slade turned to Bob, "Right Bob, now when Alison gets in we'll need you two to help with..."

"Sure, happy to help for the next half hour Jim..."

"What do you mean?"

"According to AlbionForward my scheduled finish time today is 12.30."

"Oh come on Bob this is urgent for the convention. We will need you to help with ..."

"Sorry Jim, I'll work my socks off until 12.30 and I'll meet my output targets for this morning. But then I'm off to spend time with the family. Please tell Mr Yates that according to the system, my time is my time."

* * *

A few moments later Maggie returned with defiance plastered across her face.

"Right. Obviously the convention must go ahead, and equally obvious is that we don't have any bloody furniture. So I've booked the Town Hall up the road at considerable expense to Albion. They have their main hall already set up from a do yesterday, they're just cleaning it up. It's not the ideal layout but there's no time to change it, and we're desperate."

"Wonderful," said Hasna.

"Now Hasna, we'll need to set up a meet and greet station here, get enough of our team to escort clients across to the venue. It's not ideal, but we must try."

"Surely we'll need to set up a meet and greet at the Town Hall, so we'll be spread too thin to escort people across as well."

"Yeah I take your point. Okay, you stay here with a few bodies, just offer an initial greet and then point them the right way. Get some welcome materials to hand out. We'll do the convention name badges when we do the main greet at the Town Hall."

Hasna jotted some quick notes.

Maggie turned to the new security guy. "Now look. Tell your people all I need them to do, if they can manage it, is to smile and point. Leave everything else to Hasna and the little team who will station themselves here. Don't play with the lifts, or the burglar alarms, and ask your people to try to go an hour without looking at their phones or chewing gum, until all our guests are in the Town Hall. If any of your people are asked, they will say the venue is 150 yards up the road on the left. They just have to smile and point. Got that, just smile and point..."

"We're not stupid."

"No. No you're not. But we're relying on you."

"You can trust us," said the new security guy suddenly raising his posture tall. "Trust us totally innit."

"Uhm," said Maggie. "Now Salvo, the Town Hall staff are checking over the main area as we speak. Can we serve some welcome refreshments in the Town Hall lobby? I need you to pull rabbits out of the hat like you did on Monday."

"Sorry Maggie, I can't be flexible like I was on Monday. I'm a supplier nowadays working to a contract. I can add it to the order but I'm told you'll have to tell Granwick first and then they place the order with me."

"Oh yes of course. Hasna will you get on to Granwick with that now please."

"Sure."

"Doesn't authorisation with Granwick have to come from the budget holder," said Slade.

"Argh!" exclaimed Maggie, "right yes of course, thanks Jim. I'll get on to them."

"Won't the recharge first have to go through Burridge and Perkins," said Hasna.

"Oh stuff Burridge and pissing Perkins!"

Arnie, Ali, and Jim spent the afternoon supporting the convention as originally rostered, except now it was in the nearby Town Hall. Late that Saturday evening, Arnie arrived back at the Albion Building and approached a tired looking Slade who was in his office slouching in recovery pose with his feet up.

Arnie tapped at the open door, "Jim, have you got a minute?"

"Sure Arnie come in."

"Well... actually there was something I wanted to say earlier, well two things really," he heard himself swallowing hard. Guilt had been eating him all afternoon.

"Go on."

"Well firstly I have a confession, I hadn't got Chartwell ready anyway today."

"Why do you say that?" Slade sat up and put his feet on the floor.

"Well so much going on. I was trying to sort it out, I really tried to..."

"Listen Arnie, I looked at it. Did you think we wouldn't check? I looked in the other day and Maggie went to check late last night. When she saw what you'd manage to achieve, she didn't want to make you feel you were being watched so discreetly slipped away. It was your gig, let the sergeant own the parade ground as they say. Old school people leadership that is. A rarity these days."

"So it...?"

"Look, don't get any illusions, if it wasn't acceptable she'd have been on your case. And I would have brought in a contractor if need be by Thursday. But you did an amazing job given the distractions, and it was more than passable. Normally we would want top notch here, passable is for second rate firms. But nothing here is top notch this week, we've been thrown upside down. You did fine. Maggie, Hasna and their teams could have performed their marketing magic in that environment no problem. And the second thing is..."

Arnie told him about the HR form.

Slade rubbed his chin. "That's not so good Arnie, not so good."

"Sorry."

"Why didn't you hand it in?"

"I kept trying and things kept happening, and then our HR department just sort of... well it just sort of vanished."

"So that's why you were on that HR floor that day?"

"Yeah."

"I see."

Arnie shuffled his feet uneasily.

"Did you lie to me Arnie?"

Arnie thought. "No Jim. No I don't think I did. Apart from maybe why I was on that floor that morning. I just didn't reveal everything until now. I wanted to be independent, to sort things out, to do well."

"Ok. Look we'll have to sort this next week. But don't do anything like that again. Now that's the end of it for now."

"Thanks Jim."

"Now take this."

"What is it?"

"It's a swipe to get in the front lobby on Monday morning. Muscorva Security have been given the boot. The entrance from now on won't be staffed, so..."

Maggie strode in and placed a wrapped object on the table in front of Arnie. "A little something," she said, "as a thank you for getting that Chartwell Suite ready against all the odds this week." She slumped into a nearby tumbler chair.

"But I thought that the suite was ..."

"I just overheard, seems you have high standards. That's the Albion way, at least it was."

Arnie opened the package to find an old fashioned vinyl LP. "Scrapper Blackwell and Leroy Carr!"

"I hope you haven't got that one?"

"No, I've not come across this one before..."

"It's out of commission, it's second hand I'm afraid. Probably issued in the 1960s from bundling together some crackling 30s recordings."

"Why thank you so much!"

"You earned it this week, how you got that suite as good as you did with all those disruptions we'll never know."

"And I thought..."

"Let that be a lesson to you, perfection is for amateurs, finding a way to get over the line is for professionals."

"Maggie's right, you did great this week," added Slade, "but it may not be enough to keep your job I'm afraid. None of us know what's in store next week. I thought I'd share that with you."

"Thanks Jim. I think."

"And I'm afraid as Chartwell wasn't used you won't get the staff bonus I promised. I already tried but AlbionForward is back up and it doesn't have a box for discretionary bonuses like that. So to make up for it I'll arrange a payment for you next week using a box I can tick. And come in a bit late on Monday as well, you've earned it, you must be exhausted. I told you that loyalty deserves loyalty."

"Thanks. And I need to order a mop Jim."

"A mop!"

"I can't quite explain it, but I just can't seem to get another one, no matter how hard I try. Perhaps it's best if I just buy a few mops on my way into work on Monday."

"We'll sort it Monday Arnie, don't worry."

Arnie took a deep breath, pride at the recognition of his efforts coursed through him yet fear of losing his job nagged as strong as ever. He walked outside to his locker room to change. With the doors open, and the empty floor, the sound resonated, and he could overhear from the other room.

"Did the convention go okay Maggie? I take it not so good?"

"Disaster Jim. The vibe was flat, we had chances of new openings today, I have a nose for these things but that's not the half of it. The renewal negotiations... just don't go there."

"Oh hell."

"It gets worse. We were going to dine the clients in the Chartwell afterwards, but the Town Hall needed to be booked in advance to stay open late. Hasna tried every restaurant in town, but none could give us enough seats at this notice on a Saturday. Some valued clients got up and left without being dined. Hasna is working on one deal and has taken a handful of people to dinner somewhere. A total embarrassing cock up. But it's the renewals Jim, the bloody renewals that are coming up, we might have blown them today, I had some brilliant pitches and angles ready, but I couldn't get their ears in the setting I'd wanted. Down the line this could cost us millions... Look I don't want to talk about it now..."

"Albion really doesn't need this does it. Are you okay Maggie?"

"No I'm not. Sometimes there's no way back from these things. I need a whiskey after the day I've had."

"Me too."

"Have you done your new performance indicators and targets yet Jim?"

"Are you kidding me. Nor those bloody stupid new staff appraisals. You?"

"Not a hope. I worked out that if I stopped and did nothing else it would take me over a week to complete those for all our team."

"Yeah I worked out something similar for my lot..."

"And Hasna and I have had to shelve loads of new business projects, even Brunel. There's no time to do our job anymore."

"Brunel?"

"An ingenious and beautifully simple marketing idea dreamed up between Hasna, Ron in Supplies, and Sue in Finance to *reward our suppliers with incentives each time they helped us drum up some new business with other companies in their supply chains. We'd already tested it, it would have been a sure winner. But impossible to operate day to day without our bloody Supplies or Finance teams behind us of course..."*

"Yeah I can see that..."

"Everything that made this job worthwhile is gone Jim. Success is now just ticking useless bloody boxes."

"Tell me about it."

"Sorry Jim, long horrid day."

"I know. C'mon Maggie, let's get out of here."

"I've never heard you say that before Jim."

"What?"

"Let's get out of here."

"No I suppose not, funny how these things creep up on you."

"That bad Jim?"

"Maggie, I just don't want to be here anymore. On Monday this job was my life, I'd run through brick walls to help. I often did. But if I could take early retirement tonight I'd go."

"Me too. I really would. I hate it here. I'm totally drained before I start each day. It's not the job itself, it's the nonstop crap from above. Before I was buzzing to get in every morning, full of ideas. Now I'd prefer to go and write my book. Hasna has had enough too, she's got a nice offer from another firm that she's going to take up. Who with half a brain wants to work under this bull?"

"Going straight home Maggie?"

"To that flat on my own to brood about this place? No way, I'm heading off to a little backstreet blues bar I know. I need to unwind. What about you?"

"Home to the wife. It's fish supper Friday, she's a devout Catholic."

"It's Saturday Jim."

"Oh my God so it is! I'm totally losing it. Did we have fish last night then? You know as a one off I may pop in the pub on the way home, just to clear my head."

There was silence for a moment as Arnie quietly closed his locker and was about to leave. Footsteps echoed as Maggie and Jim were obviously now out in the lobby near the lift. He would not emerge now, there might be awkwardness that he'd overheard.

He sat back down for a moment by his locker.

"Good of you to offer that payment for Arnie, but can you do that nowadays?"

"No Maggie, not officially. But I'll find an excuse. From now on I'm gonna do things off the record if it helps Albion. I'll do the same for Bob somehow. I let him down yesterday not keeping my promise to let him go early after all the extra hours he'd put in off his own bat. I'm trying to manage people like I always have. But you know I realised something today. When changes filter down that so disrupt work on the ground, it's up to our level to try to find workarounds to somehow keep the show on the road until maybe one day sanity returns."

"Even if you can get into trouble for it?"

"Who else can do it Maggie?"

Arnie walked up the pebbled path at the front of the building after Jim and Maggie had gone. It was sad to overhear how crushed they were, they were good people. He gave a tired sigh, only one day off and he would have to be back here on Monday. He knew how Maggie felt. Lucy's voice entered his head, laughing at him for messing up again. *Oh Arnie, what have you done now...*

He stopped. Something wasn't right about Lucy's voice

this time. Two managers had just said he had done great. And in his hand he had a lovely gift as a work thank you. This week he had organised his own work, overcome everything that had been thrown at him, tried hard, shown initiative to solve all sorts of things, stuck at it ... and right... and he had shown integrity by owning up.

Yes he had done all that.

You know what Lucy...

He plopped down onto the grass his mind in a whirl. Yes he had done all that, and yes he was liked.

Yes Lucy I am liked! He repeated the thought aloud.

He lay back on the lawn, his head spinning more. But surely Lucy couldn't be wrong. She was always right about him, wasn't she? On the other hand, yes he could do things, he damn well could.

And he had.

He took several deep breaths. *You know Lucy, if I am rubbish then fine, but I am my own rubbish. So to hell with your opinion of me.*

He got out his phone and hesitated for a second. Then he deleted all Lucy's texts.

Boy that felt good!

He got to his feet, no matter how bad things got in the future he would never let her soul-eating words echo around his head anymore. He puffed out his chest and resumed walking.

Upright, head up.

He reached the end of the path, and clutching the gift tightly, he skipped up the green bank, this time to the left of the path not the right as usual. Odd he had broken the habit of the last five days by going a different way.

The fear of losing his job next week was as strong as

ever, but even if that did happen, at least he had done all he could.

From his waist high perch he stood upright and gazed back at the Headquarters of the Greater Albion Bay Company. Only the top 4 floors were lit, the bottom 5 layers were now in silent darkness. The thought came back to him and made his stomach turn.

For how much longer would he last here?

BOARDROOM, FLOOR 9...

"How the hell did this happen!" Devoux stared at the three faces before him, thunder on his brow.

Friedman and Yates dropped their heads. They were all sitting with their summer coats on as the top floor air con had settled itself on maximum and could not be adjusted or switched off.

"I have a report here from Maggie Campbell in Marketing," added Devoux, "her figures on the estimated downward adjustment to our projections are dire. And just as we are negotiating lease deals for our remaining sites."

"Early days of course," said a shivering Yates. "Initial indicators would seem to suggest, and I really don't want us to adopt a blame culture here, but clearly the root of any solution would lie on the floors below."

"Hear, hear," said Friedman pulling his collar up against the air con chill. "It seems the skill set of our middle management is rather challenged with enacting our modernisation, leading them to rather disrupt our normal operations."

"Luckily we have AlbionForward," Yates added, "it is probing the web pages our managers looked at to see what we can glean. It should tell us a lot."

"I doubt it. I understand it was down for half the day," said Greta.

"Well thankfully we have our array of reforms in place this week to help operations," said Friedman. "We set out to remove barriers to performance and so far that is exactly what we have achieved."

"Yes I suppose there is an element of good fortune that this happened under our sound management," added Yates. "And we are working hard with Exemplary People1st right now to ascertain which change management model will best help smooth our

modernisation further. They've whittled it down to Senior's Hard Change, Senior's Soft, the Burke-Litwin, the EFQM, Prosci's ADKAR, or McKinskey's Seven S's."

The air con made another loud buzzing noise, then gave out some spluttering sounds before settling down again.

"So if you're both right," asked Greta staring at each of them in turn, "why are we taking this enormous hit now when we've been performing so well in recent years?"

Yates cleared his throat and read from his tablet. "We are working hard with partners, stakeholders, and other agencies to ascertain the full facts so that lessons can be learned that will enable us to build on the successes of the past and at the same time establish how we may best go forward in the future."

Friedman chipped in. "With regards to Muscorva Security, it seems that them sending some of their people to secure the park concert might have interrupted their staff continuity here to our disadvantage. But I am afraid that as they maintained their overall staff numbers here as stipulated in their contract, they did not actually break the deal with us."

"So you're saying we can't touch them!" exclaimed Greta.

Friedman leaned forward. "Difficult. It seems the root of the problem was the nature of the contract we drew up with them. Might have been a bit rushed. But Muscorva were a bit sharp too maybe."

"...a bit sharp is putting it mildly," Greta said. "To use a collo-quial term Mr Friedman, they ripped us off."

"Ah well, that's one of the risk factors in dealing with sharper outside companies," beamed Friedman. "It sharpens us up too. And Muscorva are gone now anyway."

Greta glared. "And I suppose we had to pay them to go away as well?"

"Very challenging to get all outsourcing spot on first time,"

said Friedman, "bound to be some leakage. And you know, in a way we have to respect them for their enterprise."

"Tell me we've had no leakages within the payroll." Devoux glared.

"Absolutely not!" declared Friedman.

"Not even a tiny fraction Mr Devoux!" said Yates. "That would be unforgiveable."

"Hear, hear," said Friedman, "we have our internal staff regulated till the pips squeak. And just to be extra sure we're paying a huge surplus to Burridge and Perkins to have their auditors double down on them as from next week. Even if we only save pennies it's money well spent. I assure you that any leakages we might have will only be via outsourced partners or through sourcing our contracts."

"Good. That's the way it should be," said Devoux.

Greta cut in. "And why did we outsource catering at such an inopportune time before the convention?"

"Ah well," began Friedman, "nobody's fault really. The outsourcing team on this floor are working to their own performance indicators around promptness, the convention wasn't really something they considered."

"Pleased to say they hit all their targets though," added Yates chirpily.

"Indeed they did," gloated Friedman.

"But at a cost to the rest of Albion," Greta was staring them down. "Can't you see how fragmented we have become?"

"Modernisation always presents challenges, Mrs Rutherford..."

"And it's rather inward looking," Greta added.

Yates blinked quickly and stared at the wall.

Eventually Friedman cleared his throat. "While it seems that the remaining staff did reveal their shortcomings, we must also acknowledge there may have been some unforeseen 'grey areas' with the outsourcing. A few things might have slipped down the gaps between our excellent new partners as to who does what. Perhaps some of them were adjusting to their new working environment. But apart from that the reform programme is going well."

"Going well? We are freezing in here and can barely hear ourselves think. How on earth can our staff be both flexible to respond to what needs doing each day, and at the same time chase bucket loads of targets. It might sound fine in theory. Plus we've the lost brilliant new business ideas like Brunel, gone because they involved our different departments working together. Add to that the lost business opportunities today. Have you not seen the revised downward projections?"

Yates rubbed his head.

There was a long silence as the portraits of generations of successful figures gazed down on them.

"It's a different world now Mrs Rutherford," said Friedman. "We must modernise to compete against new challenges. But you have a point that the present situation has clearly been shown to need modification."

"Yes I agree," said Yates.

"Indeed gentlemen," Greta gasped, a hint of a smile at last appearing.

"I want solutions," said Devoux who had been staring at the conversation through squinting, unblinking eyes.

"I have three, Mr Devoux," said Friedman.

"Restoring our winning teams on the ground I trust? Then just let them get on with it."

"No Mrs Rutherford. Modernisation is the right course. But from now on we will progress from internal markets to staff bidding for their own work against externals. That's what went wrong, they were clearly far too comfortable to respond to the demands of the convention. They weren't hungry enough."

"Indeed," said Yates.

Greta stared at Friedman.

"Secondly, to solve the fragmentation that you mention, no Mrs Rutherford, we will not hire back our troops. Instead we will hire in a larger team of senior managers to oversee and co-ordinate all our excellent new outside partners."

"Excellent," beamed Yates.

The air con made several loud hissing sounds, then whirred down to a silence as it packed up altogether.

"And your third proposal Mr Friedman?" said Devoux.

"Well I do acknowledge that some of the contracts may have been slightly flawed. So this new beefed up senior management team will need the most up to date information at its fingertips. We need outside experts who can drill down to find our strengths, as well as our key areas of development."

"Go on," Devoux was staring impassively.

"We need to hire in consultants."

MONDAY DAY 7

Arnie swiped his entry card and walked across the deserted lobby to the lift, his footsteps echoing in the deserted cavern. Roger's cheery greeting amidst the hustle and bustle seemed a lifetime ago.

He needed to stay positive if he was to try and keep this job. And he had bought three mops from the store on the way in. Obstacles were not going to stop him working hard today.

He checked the phone, nothing from Lucy. Never mind. He would text her tonight to wish her well, tomorrow was the anniversary of the day they had met. No way would he allow her criticisms to fill his head anymore, but that was no reason to be uncivilised.

Upstairs at his locker Arnie changed into his torn work overalls. With the Chartwell task out of the way it was time to see what Jim wanted him to do now. He entered the office where Bob was sorting some tools on his cluttered desk and Ali was on her knees rummaging in a cupboard across the room.

"Morning Arnie," said Bob. Ali turned and waved her hand in greeting.

"Morning guys, is Jim about?"

"Yeah somewhere, he was doing a tour of the building to see what jobs need doing," answered Bob.

"Writing them specs I suppose," added Ali.

Arnie heard footsteps approaching, he turned to speak to Jim, but it was Friedman who walked in.

Friedman scanned the scene before him in silence for a moment. "Is Mr Slade about?" he eventually asked.

"I was just saying he's touring the building," repeated Bob.

"What are you doing here?"

"Me?

"Yes you."

"I work here."

"Still?"

"Excuse me?"

"You mean to say you are still based here, next to Mr Slade's office?"

"I've always sat here, this has been my cubbyhole for years. And Ali is in the next one."

"You'll both have to move."

"Pardon?"

"You can't sit here, Mr Slade is the client manager. He has to allocate jobs to the best bidder."

Ali and Bob exchanged a puzzled look.

"...and you are the in-house staff trying to win those very deals if I'm not mistaken."

"Win the deals? I thought we just priced them, an internal market you said."

"It's an external market now. From today you must

compete with outside firms for every task that Slade sets. If you overprice, Mr Slade must use outsiders."

"What...?"

"So you can't be based beside him. It's far too incestuous. Gives you a competitive advantage over the others."

"From what I can see we already have a competitive advantage over the others," said Ali looking up, "we know what we're doing."

Friedman gave a sickly grin. "You'll both have to move immediately. Find another location. I'm astonished to find this sloppiness. Uncompetitive behaviour you know."

"Do you know how much gear we have Mr Friedman," said Ali, "moving that lot will put us out of action for half a day."

"You best get started then. You can both move to the basement until we decide what to do with that space."

"The basement!" Bob sat upright.

"From now on that can be your base from which you bid to win jobs up here. And from next week you'll be a separate organisation, the Albion Bay Services Company." Friedman turned to Arnie who was adjusting stuff on his trolley.

Arnie nodded a nervous greeting.

"And what the hell are you doing here?"

"Me?"

"Yes you!"

"My locker and trolley live next door."

"Oh it gets worse."

"Pardon?"

"You will have to relocate too. You must all separate, too much working together going on. Resistance to change that's what this is, resistance to change. Move immediately to... well I dunno where... move to somewhere on your own, not with these two. You could be in healthy competition bidding for work against them where your skills overlap. Go anywhere else really. Ask Mr Slade where the hell we should put you."

"Oh for heaven's sake, this is total b..."

"...don't say it Bob," said Ali.

Friedman turned to go muttering to himself. "Sitting beside the client manager, the very idea. Oh my," he scoffed with a chuckle, "I'll repeat this tale at dinner parties, whatever next. In-house contractors sitting next to the client manager. Oh my..."

"Well it is total bollocks," said Bob when the sound of the departing chortling had receded.

"I know it is," said Ali, "but just watch what you say. These new people are prickly. C'mon we'd better get packing up our stuff then. This will take us all morning."

Arnie's phone went, it was Slade. "Arnie, come up to top floor right away."

"Sure Jim, but shall I finish moving my locker first? Mr Friedman told us all to relocate."

"Indeed Arnie. Come to me first, then do that."

"Hey Jim," Bob said taking the phone from Arnie. "Ali and me are moving all our gear too, it could take us all morning."

"I know Bob, listen ping me a text when you're done and are ready to bid for work again. In the meantime I'll have to use outside firms to do some jobs while you're tied up," Slade's voice lowered, "but listen I'll keep some of the bigger ones back until you two are in the game again. So text me straight away when you're available so I can get some work to you both today. Got that, good."

Arnie heard the click of Slade hanging up.

"I wonder if my locker would balance on my trolley," said Arnie rubbing his chin.

"Doubt it, but we've got a pallet trolley to carry that," said Ali.

"No way," said Bob.

"What do you mean?"

"No way are we helping Arnie move."

"Bob, what in God's name...?"

"Arnie is the enemy now. Didn't you just hear that he could be in competition with us now, bidding for our jobs. So the longer he is tied up and out of the game while he is sorting himself out the better for us. If we ain't viable earning money into our budgets, well it's obvious what will happen to us. And I've got a young family to feed..."

"Don't worry, I understand," said Arnie. "I think."

"Look mate, I know it's bollocks but whereas last week we started as *all for one* ...well that changed to *every man for himself*. Well from today from what Friedman says it's *dog eat dog*."

* * *

On the top floor Arnie exited the lift and gasped.

Wow! This was a different world. Dark wood panelling bedecked the walls, ornate marble decorated the arches around the lobby, signs in gold leaf on dark wood directed towards 'Boardroom' to the right and 'Executive Offices' to the left. Arnie pushed through a heavy wooden door toward Executive Offices and after walking up a mahogany panelled corridor he encountered a small lobby area from which several doors emerged. Arnie paused, there was something olde world and hallowed about the vibe in these wood bedecked walls and ceilings.

It made you want to whisper.

Slade soon came bowling out of one of the doors. "Ah

Arnie, excellent. Right, so basically up here will require your full attention each morning from now on. With you busy with the Chartwell last week it kinda got neglected. And you will have to keep the Traders' Rooms nice on our floor below. Got that, good."

"Sure Jim."

"Any questions?"

"It's rather warm up here."

"It is rather warm," Slade mopped his brow. "Air con has packed up. Anyway that is going to be your morning's work from now on. Floors 8 and 9 are all that's left of Albion."

"So Maggie and Hasna are...?"

"Gone. And all their marketing team. We'll be using an outside marketing consultant from now on. We don't extract, make or process anything anymore. We're basically about finance, trading and leasing, so as I said before, you'll probably have some extra lease managers up on these floors to look after."

"Oh right..."

"Now, we're gonna be letting out all the lower floors to other firms for their office space. Some of the companies managing our remaining overseas sites might take a floor or two. Mr Friedman says it's part of his plan to keep things together."

"Okay, and Floor 6, Chartwell?"

"It'll be let out as well. A shame to smash up all those lovely art deco features but there we are. And you will be our guy keeping floors 1 to 7 nice for the tenants. Got that, good."

"Er okay. So where will I be based? I'm told I have to move ...?"

"Oh yeah. Um...look we don't have anywhere for you now," Slade rubbed his chin. "Look base your locker and trolley in the Pioneers Room, Floor 5 for now. We'll be getting the lowest floors ready for letting out first and working our way up."

"Ok so…"

"… so down on Floor 2 today there'll be sub-contractors working around you, putting in partitions and entry doors and the like. Got that, good."

"Yeah I think so."

"Good. Now go into that room there and wait. I'll just make a quick call first."

Arnie entered a wood panelled room where a woman was sitting on a chair by an open window letting in cool fresh air.

"Hey Arnie!"

"Sue! I thought you'd left?"

"I have. I mean I had."

"So you're…"

"I'm here as a consultant to help with drawing up the deals, they said I knew the business. Odd really, after leaving I set up a management consultancy with Sandeep and then bingo, Albion called to hire us. I've no section to manage yet the fee is huge. But there we are."

"Oh good for you Sue."

"It is really. And Sandeep will be in tomorrow. Lots of other consultants coming in too I'm told. How are you anyway, any news on you and Lucy?"

"No Sue, no news…"

"Aw I really am sorry Arnie…" Sue broke off as another figure entered. Sue let out a mini shriek. "Maggie!"

"Not just me Sue." Behind Maggie entered Ron and Salvo who was carrying a tray of sandwiches. Jim followed, putting his phone away.

"How great to see you all," said Sue. But…" she gazed at

Jim before addressing the room, "I'm a bit confused. I'm only here as a consultant and..."

"Well I'm here as a contractor now," said Salvo. "My firm does the catering for Albion." He started handing out some sandwiches on a tray.

"I'm agency," said, Fleetwood walking in wearing a Stevie Nicks T-shirt. "Yates outsourced our IT but I got a job working for Bespoke-Forward who won the IT deal here. Naturally they sent me back to do the support as I know the AlbionForward system."

"I'm here as the marketing consultant," said Maggie taking a sandwich. "I've been hired to give a good spin on leasing out this building's floor space. Suits me as it's one day a week and I want to write my book. Silly money for what I'm doing. What about you Ron?"

"I'm rehired," said Ron munching on some of Salvo's side salad, "as a senior client executive to pull the contractors together. The salary they're paying, well I could only dream about when I worked here, and I've no staff to manage. And there's more time for me fishing."

"Good to see you back here Ron," said Sue.

Ron sniffed. "Well I guess I'll have my hands full. Already I'm booked out all afternoon at Granwick to see what's going on." He gave a wry smile, "Herewith, for the purposes of..."

The room erupted in laughter.

Apart from Slade who addressed the room. "As you're all not Albion staff nowadays, I'm afraid that Mr Friedman says you won't have your own desks or any office space. It's going to be tight all round as Albion only lives in floors 8 and 9 now, and we also have lots of new change consultants coming in today. They will have to sit somewhere. So I've arranged hot desks for you to share on the days when you come in. They'll be beside me downstairs on Floor 8 in Bob's and Ali's old cubbyholes. Mr Friedman has moved the technicians away from there so I figured the space could be put to use. Bob and Ali are clearing their stuff out right now."

There was an awkward silence.

Slade cleared his throat and turned to Arnie, "Right then Arnie, come with me."

Arnie followed Slade out of the room.

"Right, before you start work, here's your payslip. The money should go into your bank by 10 a.m. on the fourth Monday of every month. It's company tradition, the founders were Methodists back in the day and figured it was better to pay the staff on a Monday morning rather than at the end of the week as the staff were less likely to drink the lot. I'm not sure it ever worked but there we are."

"Great!"

"You've earned it. Funny thing is, we all got ours electronically via Exemplary People1st but you've got the old fashioned Albion paper one. So check it, and if it's not right let me know. Oh and best check it's gone into your bank too as you seem to be the odd one out."

Arnie opened the slip and eagerly scanned the amounts, "Yeah Jim, it seems in order."

"It's just gone 10 o'clock so check your bank to see it's there."

"Sure, I can check on my phone app here."

Arnie tapped into his phone. His bank's app opened, and Arnie stared frozen waiting for it to load.

Yippee, he had a pay cheque! It was only for one week this month, but it was a real pay cheque!

"Arnie?"

Earned money in his bank account again! At long last!

"Arnie?"

Oh my! He would sure mention this to Lucy when he texted her later, so who was a forty something useless nobody then...

"Arnie?"

He caught himself. Begone from me head Lucy! Begone!

"ARNIE!!!"

"Er yeah, sorry Jim... er yep, it's all gone through. It says it's from the Greater Albion Bay Company."

"From the Greater Albion Bay Company you say?"

"That's right."

"How strange. How very strange."

* * *

Later that morning Arnie completed his tasks upstairs, logged his progress on AlbionForward and went down to relocate his stuff.

He entered the office and did a double take. Ali's cubbyhole was piled high with stuff being packed up, but in Bob's former workspace flesh was being squeezed.

Sue and Ron were sharing a chair looking at a computer screen, each had one cheek of their bums on the seat and the other off. Fleetwood was sitting on the floor with his knees bent swiping a tablet, Maggie was sitting on a toolbox, and Salvo was standing squashed by the cubbyhole's entrance. Outside Bob's cubbyhole there was crashing and banging as Ali and Bob were charging backwards and forwards with trollies, manically emptying their cupboards and loading gear into piles of boxes and paladins.

Arnie jumped back as Bob wheeled a small trolley in front of him, and then leaped forward as Ali wheeled something coming the other way. It was scary here, the consultants were clearly keeping out of the way.

"Hey Arnie," said Bob as he shot by with another loaded trolley, "all this sweat and what the hell are we achieving eh? Listen mate, sorry about earlier. Of course we'll help you move your locker in a bit, I'm not going to lower myself to this bollocks. It's funny how their thinking creeps up on you, gets you behaving that way without you knowing it. We need to get packed up first though, and we gotta be bloody quick. I've got a family to feed so we've gotta get back in the game before some outsiders nick our jobs."

"That would be great Bob."

"Beep, beep," said Ali with a smile as she whizzed the other side of Arnie with a paladin trolley.

Arnie jumped again.

Bob stopped to wipe his brow and surveyed the shelving and racks on the wall holding all the tools. "You know Ali," he said catching his breath, "we really need to take those wall fittings with us to house all this gear when we get down in the basement. Any idea where we last left that special screwdriver for those fittings?"

"In your desk, top drawer."

Bob went to his overpopulated former cubbyhole. "Excuse me," Bob said to Salvo as he tried to edge sideways to get in.

"Sorry," said Salvo, turning side on and placing a foot outside.

Ali whizzed past with another trolley carrying a cabinet. Salvo quickly withdrew his foot.

"Blimey that was close," said Salvo. "It's a bit dangerous out there, I'm staying in here."

Bob attempted to squeeze passed Salvo again into his cubbyhole.

"Can we pass you something Bob?" asked Sue manoeuvring herself.

"No Sue, the desk drawer is locked with my pin, I'll only be a sec if I can just stretch in past you all."

Arnie gazed at the scene. Bob finally squeezed his torso past Salvo, planting his forward leg on Fleetwood's foot.

"Ouch!"

"Sorry mate."

Fleetwood shifted. Bob had it seems finally found a piece of bare floor to put down his front foot. But he was still only halfway to his desk, and his trailing foot was sticking out around Salvo, now dangling in the air. Bob leaned forward further, pivoting from the waist as he tottered across Fleetwood's raised knees and Sue's shoulder, reaching off balance into the throng.

"Sorry can I just..." said Bob stretching out his arm for all his might towards his desk drawer.

"Sorry," said Maggie pivoting on the toolbox to give Bob room.

"Ouch," said Fleetwood again.

"Sorry," said Bob.

"Sorry," said Sue leaning sideways into Ron.

"Sorry," said Ron leaning into the partition as far as he could.

"Fucking hell!" yelled Bob. "You can't even get to a screw-driver for bloody consultants everywhere."

* * *

The morning flew by. After sweating buckets to make quick progress, then stopping for an hour to complete their risk assessments, they finally managed to move all their gear.

Time to get back in the game!

Arnie exited the lift on Floor 2 to get his new instructions from Jim. Bob and Ali were close behind. They crossed the lift lobby and reached the entrance to the main area.

Ahead the noise was deafening, drills were buzzing amidst shouts, sawing, banging, workstations, and stepladders. Around the whole floor where Sue and Accounts had once been were clusters of strangers putting in partitions and entry doors and the like.

"Where's Jim?" shouted Ali as she reached Arnie.

"I can't see him," yelled Arnie peering through the throng of separate workstations, "lets hunt him down."

They each grabbed a hard hat and a high viz bib that were laid out and started to zig zag their way through the floor.

"Did you update AlbionForward that we'd finished moving?" yelled Ali above the noise of a nearby electric saw.

"No I forgot, best we go back and do it," shouted Arnie.

"Oh bollocks to it," screamed Bob as he passed a noisy drill, "let's just find Jim."

They reached the other side of the large office space through the hordes of workers.

No sign of Jim.

At the other end the three stopped. Arnie gazed out of the window, on the front lawn below were dozens of people lying about. A few men and women had a ball and were having a kickabout.

"What's all this?" asked Arnie.

"They must be zero hours casuals hoping to get some work with these subcontractors," answered Ali.

"Hey," said Bob pointing outside, "look who's down there."

"Who, where?" asked Ali.

"Down there," Bob pointed.

"Can't see who you're pointing at?"

"Right there on the bottom step, the tall guy with the black beanie hat. He's the one that used to work with Ron. I'm sure it's him. He was our Albion darts champion. The fella who helped us save the deal last week by remembering what fittings to use."

"Oh yeah, that's him. Aw look at him now," said Ali.

"Nobody knows our past supplies solutions better than him," said Bob, "what a waste."

"I wonder if he knows Ron was upstairs this morning in a sharp suit," asked Ali. "Seems such a waste, a good team being split both ways like that."

"And look there," said Bob.

"Where?" asked Ali.

"Down there, near the darts guy."

"Where?"

"Him with the clipboard. Isn't that Maz the security fella. He seems to be taking people on."

"What's it got to do with him?"

"Buggered if I know."

"C'mon," said Bob, "let's try again to find Jim. Then maybe we can actually start work today."

They snaked their way back through more workstations and eventually found Jim in the middle of the floor talking to a young guy who had his baseball cap on backwards.

"...I said I wanted a decorator," said Slade.

"I am a decorator."

"But this morning you said you were a carpet fitter?"

"I am a carpet fitter."

"You've just turned your baseball cap the other way around."

"That's right. Maz took me on downstairs for both jobs, and as a carpenter."

"But you don't even have a saw."

"Well I thought…"

"Now listen…" Slade broke off on seeing the three arrive. "Ah good you're ready to go again. Right, before I forget, you'll each need to do peer reviews later, new instructions from Mr Yates. You know observing and feeding back on each other's work and so on."

"But we don't have time to do any work," said Ali.

"I hear you Ali. Mr Yates was made aware of the new time pressures. His response is that he's hired in an online training company to deliver a whole day course on *organising and planning workloads.*"

"Is he from this planet?" said Bob.

"And don't forget the other online courses he wants you to finish by the end of the week."

"Will all these have to do this stuff as well?" Ali said as she pointed to the clusters of casuals and subcontractors.

"Doubt it."

"Doesn't seem fair. We're supposed to compete against them before we can do anything, yet we have to jump through all these extra hoops as well."

"It's total bollocks."

Slade gave a weary smile. "You see over there where Mr Friedman is talking to that trader near the exit to the lobby? Go and hang around somewhere about there. I'll be right over in a minute, I've got some jobs you can price up and bid for."

The three made their way back towards the entrance, passed more step ladders where contractors were doing electrics in the ceiling.

"Our Work Prevention Teams upstairs are having a bloody field day today," muttered Bob as they walked. "Totally ridiculous… hey, who's putting that partition in over there?"

"Dunno," answered Arnie following Bob's gaze...

"Just look at the state of that. That won't stay up, he's making a proper bodge job of it. That ain't safe."

The three reached the entrance by the lobby where Friedman could be overheard talking to the heavily hair gelled trader, "...*but essentially our change management consultants today whittled it down to us using either McKinskey's Seven S's or Kotter's Eight Steps.....*"

"Excuse me, Mr Friedman..."

"What do you want?" said the hair gelled trader.

"Mr Friedman, that partition over there won't hold."

"I don't have time," Friedman said turning back to the trader.

"But Mr Friedman, these jobs are being botched."

"They meet company standards."

"They can't do."

"We've adjusted the snagging time for jobs to be perfected after they're finished. Look on AlbionForward."

"To how long?"

"Three years."

"Three years!"

"That's what I said."

"But Albion's longest time to put snags right after completion has always been a fortnight. Even for our bigger jobs."

"The consultants already proposed a solution. You're behind the curve. It's what we pay them huge bucks for. From today, only jobs outside the three years snagging time will count as failing to meet standards. Read your emails. All staff were consulted. You had a fifteen minute window to present your views this morning."

Friedman and the hair gelled trader started to head across the lobby towards the lift.

"So are we all supposed to drop our work to these standards?" said Bob running alongside them. Arnie and Ali followed.

"Same high standards as always at Albion. We've simply adjusted the snagging time for the job to be perfected."

"But some of this is not safe, so standards have dropped."

Friedman stopped. "On the database 100% of jobs are now up to standard within the snagging time, a huge improvement over the figures which were previously at 92%. So standards have gone up."

"You gotta be kidding..."

"Check for yourself. There's a full breakdown on Albion-Forward under our new 'Info Sharing and Staff Openness' tab. It's on there, so it's true."

"But this is..."

"Now I suggest you get bidding if the in-house team wants work. Otherwise ..."

"Mr Friedman, we've got a bouncer down there hiring chippies who don't own a saw..."

"He is now subcontracted by Exemplary People1st to hire casuals for us..."

"This is all total b..."

"...now you look," the hair gelled trader leaned in on Bob as Friedman got into the lift and held the door open, "we don't have time for this. Speak to your line manager if you have concerns. You menial workers being outsourced is the future. So I suggest you learn to adapt, and quickly."

The trader followed Friedman into the lift, stood directly facing Bob with a deliberate wide Alpha pose, smirked as he chewed on his gum, and hit the lift button.

The lift doors slid closed.

And then half opened again. Then they juddered open

and shut several times to the obvious frustration of the trader who had lost his smirk and was now jabbing madly at a lift button and cursing the electrics. Finally the lift doors closed properly.

"What a load of total fucking bollocks," Bob yelled, pacing back and forth across the lobby. "And I should have decked that smarmy twat."

Arnie put his hand on his shoulder.

"Shush now Bob," Ali grabbed his arm, "you've overdone it already, are you after being sacked..."

" ...but we look like we're doing things on the cheap."

"Ach, of course we're doing things on the cheap."

"I tell ya this place is..."

"Do you wanna know what I think Bob?" said Ali.

"I'm all ears."

"From what I can see, they want to change things but they haven't got the first clue how to go about it. They think they know what they're doing but they don't. So long as things can be sorted on a spreadsheet, go on a website, or put in a contract, all is well. They understand that. They can see it. But all the hidden things that grease the wheels and save time and money, like you fixing something in your own time to help win a deal, well it don't tick a box. They can't see it and so they don't get it. So it doesn't count."

"Are they that fucking stupid?"

"It's the way it is now Bob."

"So what are we supposed to do?"

"Stop caring Bob. Do the minimum they ask. Take the money home. And stop bloody caring."

* * *

That night Arnie walked up the pebbled path and stared across the litter strewn green where people had been hanging out all day. A few stoned bodies were lying about. He got out his phone and texted Lucy a happy anniversary for tomorrow and wished her well.

Leave it at that.

He trudged on up the path. As he approached the street there was a face down figure half on the pebbles and half on the lawn. He looked in a bad way, Arnie bent over to check. It was the tall man with the beanie hat.

"You alright mate?"

"Yeah I guess," the man said in a daze, "thanks."

"What you doing here at this hour?"

"I earned a few bob here today in the end."

"Want a hand up?"

"Listen, in there, in that place," he waved at the Albion Building, "my name is on the darts cup, you see, it's in there."

"Oh right. You sure you're ok?" Arnie held out a hand.

"No, er just leave me for a bit, I'll be okay. I did loads in there for years. Always gave extra. Only last week I helped save a deal you know, I knew the special fittings you see. I remembered from years ago. I was worth my weight. Ron always said I pulled my weight and more. We worked together." His eyes rolled as he lost focus. " But now he's a consultant or something and I'm a... I'm a whatever, carpenter, plumber, nobody cares what you are anymore. Turn up an' call yourself what you like. But there you are."

Arnie surveyed the lawn, there were some cheap liquor bottles dotted around and one of the bodies across the way had got up and was staggering his way home.

"He used to work for Sue Ragan in accounts," the tall man said, "he heard there was work going today. You haven't got a few quid for a bag of chips have ya?" The man had raised himself up onto his elbows.

Arnie raised an eyebrow. "Chips, yeah right."

The man looked at Arnie through unfocused, bleary eyes.

Arnie sighed. "Oh look, here mate, whatever helps get you through the day," he handed the man all the coins that he had in his pocket.

Arnie walked up the little green bank and turned to look back at the litter strewn lawn. Across the way the beanie hat was slowly staggering to his feet. Arnie gazed at the building, those lone two top floors oozing light up there seemed very detached from the darkness of the vacant floors below, and the once immaculate front lawn of the world famous Greater Albion Bay Company.

BOARDROOM, FLOOR 9...

"The report before you outlines full details," Friedman announced. "The broad summary is that external markets have been successfully introduced across all areas. Outsourcing is at an advanced stage, and the floors below us are being prepared for commercial rent as we speak. The percentage of maintenance and renovation tasks meeting company standards is, I am pleased to say, now at 100%."

"And AlbionForward is giving us live updates on staff work progress, the info capture is priceless," added Yates.

"And overseas Mr Friedman?" asked Devoux.

"All sites around the world are all now either sold off or leased out. We are absolved of all administration and responsibility. There is just one site in Alaska that we could not sell or lease out as it is not viable. It has been closed and we have hired a firm to decommission it for us. Full details in the report. We no longer extract or process anything anywhere, we are now solely a financial services and trading company."

"And staff numbers are a fraction of what they were," Yates added.

"...and are these staff numbers up to date?" asked Devoux.

"Yes Mr Devoux," answered Yates, "we just have some finance officers up here on the top floor covering a few core functions, and a few lease managers overseeing the contracts on our last global sites. Apart from that, on the floor below we have a full array of traders, then there's what's left of a few support staff. So yes, all in all a much more streamlined operation."

"Indeed," added Friedman. "And working with our new partners, outsourcing has been a huge step forward on our path to modernisation."

"Well yes outsourcing has been a huge step forward for Albion," replied Greta, "apart from the things we've recently

witnessed like the fragmentation and disruption it has caused, the lost deals, the inability to develop cross departmental business projects, the absence of initiative and proactive thinking because ground staff are no longer embedded within us, the things that have fallen down the gaps between our so-called partners, and surprise, surprise these partners naturally each focusing on their own narrower contractual obligations. Then we have the loss of on the ground familiarity, the loss of ideas from the floor, the loss of a ladder for talent to climb, and the loss of staff loyalty. Then there's the lack of flexibility through not having our own teams to deploy, the loss of organisational memory, the fact that our remaining managers are run off their feet trying to hold the show together and the knock on effects of them being so distracted, not to mention the waning of brand and company identity. And that's without the contract supervision costs, the time involved, the contract fees we are incurring, and the considerable other hidden on-costs of contracting out. Apart from that, yes Mr Friedman outsourcing at Albion has indeed been working wonderfully well."

Devoux stared into space, unblinking. "I want leaner."

"I want my objections noted, you have my report," Greta stood up and began to gather her belongings ready to walk out.

"The challenges from the Far East will not go away," replied Friedman. "We must modernise to be ready. There is no room for sentimentality."

"On that one thing Mr Friedman we agree," Greta answered, now on her feet standing behind her chair, files in her hand. "No sentimentality, I've told you that before. Do not mistake our old sound leadership and business principles for charity or senti-mentality."

Devoux also stood up. "Now here's what we will do."

Greta paused at the door as Friedman and Yates looked on from their seats.

"Mr Friedman and Mr Yates; from today you no longer work together."

The two glanced at each other and then back to Devoux.

"It's time real competition visited both of you too."

Friedman swallowed hard and ran his index finger inside his collar. Yates blinked rapidly several times, took off his large glasses, wiped them, put them back on, and then took them off again.

Devoux stared dispassionately, standing motionless, eyes like slits through rimless glasses. "From now on you will each lead a separate team made up of some of our remaining senior staff. We will see which team can perform the last leg of our outsourcing and modernisation to best effect. Your teams are not to communicate with each other. There will be a huge monetary bonus for the team that outsources the most successfully. What we want is a lean core business running a huge array of outsourced contracts, you understand me, a lean modernised core business."

Greta Rutherford slammed the door behind her.

TUESDAY DAY 8

The next morning Arnie walked up the pebbled path on his way in to work. He looked at the lawn and did a double take, today it was strangely empty.

Odd. There were no early bird casuals hanging about hoping for work. The partition jobs must be on hold today, it could be the only explanation. Arnie swiped in and crossed the lobby, the place was very quiet today.

Deathly quiet.

And no reply from Lucy on his phone either, oh well. He went to Floor 5 and changed into his torn overalls in the Pioneers Room. He sure was isolated down here, it was strange not being up near Jim and the others on Floor 8.

Come to think of it, in the whole building he hadn't seen a human face yet this morning.

He exited the Pioneers Room and wheeled his trolley across the sea of grey office carpet where some department or another had once been. He couldn't remember which one anymore. He called the lift, he would head up to Jim's office to find out what he was meant to do on the top two floors this morning.

He got out of the lift at Floor 8 and paused. The door to Building Services was wide open.

What...!

Inside, the place looked like it had been cleaned out by locusts.

He edged in. The desktop computers were gone and everything else, just Jim's desk and some chairs were left dotted about. He gazed across at Bob's former cubbyhole, odd there were no consultants about anywhere today. Arnie got out his phone to call Slade.

"Hi Jim, it's Arnie. Where is everyone, there's nobody about?"

"I'm down in the lobby Arnie. Bob and Ali are with me, we're all just about to leave the building. Where are you?"

"I've just come to see you and..."

"Have you not had a letter?"

"No, what letter?"

"Your redundancy letter, there's an email version too."

"No, I've had nothing."

"Check your email again."

"Okay Jim," Arnie checked on his phone. "No nothing here."

"Are you sure you gave the firm your correct email address?"

"Sure, my appointment letter is in this inbox and I'm just checking... there's nothing in my AlbionForward mailbox either."

"How odd. Look, we've all been made redundant in Building Services, plus all the traders, and lease managers, everyone that was left on the top two floors basically. Apparently all our jobs have been outsourced, although I've no idea which company is taking over the duties. Nor where they are."

"But I've not received anything."

"Weird."

"What shall I do?"

"Hang on Arnie... you did say you got your payslip from Albion yesterday?"

"That's right."

There was a silence.

"Are you still there Jim?"

"Sorry Arnie just thinking it through. Look our redundancy notices were all issued by Exemplary People1st, and our redundancy pay outs are from them too."

"So...?"

"Well they also issued all our payslips yesterday. Yet yours came from Albion, right?"

"Yeah, and it said from the Greater Albion Bay Company on my bank statement."

"And you said you didn't hand in that form last week to transfer your employment details?"

"I tried to but things kinda happened."

"Never mind. Look, what I think has happened here is that when the Exemplary People1st took over the new staff system you weren't on their list, because you didn't hand in that form to transfer your details. So in short, these new people can't send you something to end your employment because they don't know you exist."

"I think I follow Jim."

"So your details are still on what's left of the old Albion computer system. Some backup account must still be auto generating your monthly pay slip. That can be the only explanation. Do you understand?"

"I think so."

"Right, now all the senior management have also gone including Devoux, Friedman, Greta, Yates, and all the others. So there's nobody left to ask."

"How? Was the company sold?"

"No, not as far as we know. In truth I've no idea what's happened. Yates emailed to tell me they were all gone on the top floor too. So there's nobody left in Albion to hire in the consultants, or to take on the casuals or sub-contractors."

"But in that case..."

"Arnie, it simply doesn't make sense but there we are. As we are all redundant, I guess we will never know now. But if there are no lease managers the lower floors won't be let out either. It seems that after over a century and a half of success, you are the last employee of the world famous Greater Albion Bay Company."

"Scary."

"I bet."

"What shall I do?"

There was another silence.

"Jim?"

"Sorry Arnie I'm just thinking it through. Right now, listen carefully, I mean very carefully. If due to this computer glitch you have not yet had your employment terminated, that is no fault of yours. They should have set up more robust systems. Keep taking the pay until some-body gives you the termination you are entitled to. Until that time, I guess, you are still legally and properly employed. Got that, good."

"I kinda think so."

"But thinking it through even more, that means I wouldn't give them any excuses to come back at you later for the pay you earn between now and the day they spot this mistake."

"I don't follow, what excuses?"

"It's up to you, but if I were you I'd keep turning up for work until you hear officially that you don't have a job anymore. Sooner or later, possibly in a few days, some-body in authority, whoever that now is, will walk in on you and will probably end your employment immediately. But until then you still have a job that a system is paying you for, so you may as well clock up each day's pay while you can. My set of the front door keys are in my office desk, third drawer down, the pin to open it is 1948. Got that?"

"It's very odd."

"Sure is. Now listen. I'll pass you on to Bob."

"Hey Arnie," said Bob, "now listen. After you swipe your-self into the lobby each morning the movement sensor will kick off the burglar alarm and every cop in town will be on top of you in minutes."

"So what do I ...?"

"You will have one minute to deactivate the alarms, otherwise they'll hear it at our former sites in Alaska."

"Yeah I've heard them alarms before."

"So what you do is... hang on a minute Arnie..."

"Bob...?"

"Sorry Arnie..."

"Hey mate...." Bob seemed to be shouting at somebody.

"Bob?"

'Hey mate, how's it feel to be outsourced as well eh? Menial jobs going is the future is it, but now you're crying when your turn comes eh?'

"Are you there Bob?"

"Sorry Arnie, that hair gelled trader who was snooty to me yesterday is just leaving with his boxes, he's in tears down here."

"Bob can you hear me?" Arnie strained to hear but Bob appeared to be gone again. "Bob...?"

"Aw don't cry mate. You'll be alright. Ah there, there, then. You'll soon get used to it. I suggest you learn to adapt and quickly."

"Bob are you...?"

"Hi Arnie, sorry mate, he had that coming. Ain't it funny how these prats are so cocky and aloof one minute when it's us being shat on, and suddenly how flaky they become when it's their turn to get hit. Incredible! Right then Arnie mate, go into the Intake Cupboard on the right, and on the alarm panel just tap in the latest code which is Churchill1945. It will auto-set each night unless you switch it off. Got that, you tap in Churchill1945."

"Will do thanks Bob."

"Take care mate, oh and Ali sends her love."

Slade came back on the line. "OK Arnie, Ali and Bob and all the remaining staff are already outside, and I'm exiting the building right now. As of this moment you will have the entire building to yourself. Now if I remember rightly that trophy cabinet needs to be kept nice. Got that, good."

"I'm on it Jim. Goodbye."

"Great."

"Oh and Jim..."

"Yeah."

"Well thanks for always being so decent with me."

"No problem, so long Arnie."

* * *

Arnie took a deep breath his head spinning.

He gazed at Jim's vacant office and what used to be Bob

and Ali's cubbyholes and tried to take it in. Suddenly he felt very small rattling around in this place. It was scary, spooky almost. He shook his head and rubbed his face hard with both hands, he had to stop thinking too much or he'd go nuts.

He sat down in Jim's big chair and jumped up again.

That was not his place. How dare he!

He wandered over to the nearest cubbyhole and slumped into Bob's old chair. It began to swivel around as he collected his thoughts. Jim was probably right, sooner or later, some authority figure was going to show up. And then Arnie would be redundant for sure, after all what he was doing now wasn't exactly serving anybody. It was the story of his life, the greatest loser in town. But as Jim had said, he could clock up at least a few days of pay in the meantime. He needed the money, so keeping his head down and carrying on while some stupid account was paying him was a no brainer. It's not as if he had other jobs waiting to walk into.

Hell, if he was going to be a loser, he may as well be a paid loser.

But hang on, he was no loser, that was Lucy's voice creeping in again. Hadn't Jim and Maggie praised his efforts, and Bob too. He was not just a worker here, he was part of this place. And thinking about it, he'd better be present on site when whoever it was turned up to end his contract, Jim had a point about that. And if that was the case, he'd better show he had been doing something. He would get back to work right now. What else could he do?

Sit here for days on end twiddling his thumbs?

He could think later.

Adrenalin started to run through him. He puffed out his chest, Mr Arnold Horatio Smeggins was not going to let anybody down. And maybe it would help his reputation at the next interview if he had kept the place nice, working unsupervised, that kind of thing, it must count for something.

That's settled then.

He would go down and hoover the sea of office grey tiled carpets on one of the lower floors first, then see to what used to be Salvo's canteen. Tomorrow he would make sure he got that silver shining in the trophy cabinet before tackling the old Traders' Room. A rota, yes he needed a rota of jobs to be done. He was in charge now. And it would be his own rota. Devised by him.

He sighed as he stood up. Jim, Bob and Ali were good sorts, such a shame he would never see them again. He felt the phone vibrate in his pocket. He gazed at the message, it was from Lucy on their anniversary.

At last!

His heart raced, at least some happy reminisces as a shared memory surely. Or congratulations on the job perhaps. Or asking how he was maybe. Just something like that. Anything.

Arnie, I met someone a few wks ago. I want u to know it saddens me we didn't work out. You cld have improved yourself u know. Malcolm is sexy smart clever n funny, all I ever wanted. Look after yourself, Lucy

He walked out into the lobby and slid down to the floor at the lift where once Jim had hurled his clipboard on Arnie's first day. A numbness engulfed him, it was always on the cards that she would move on of course. He was about to wish them both well, but something was cruel about her message. He would read it again. He got his phone out, and then changed his mind.

Damn it!

He hit delete.

For five minutes he sat motionless with his back to the lift staring unblinking into space.

Right, he would keep on working, dwelling on it would make him feel worse. Dwelling on anything made him feel worse.

His stomach was already hollowed out.

* * *

That night as he reached the green bank he looked back at the building. On the left side of the façade the "S" had dropped from the inscription around the huge anchor emblem and the message now read '*ince 1855*'. The sad thing was he didn't have the equipment to do anything about it, and although it was a million miles outside a janitor's job, as the last person here he surely ought to try. It looked tricky though, getting up there to sort that out.

Arnie shook his head, slumped his hands deep into his pockets, and began to trudge toward the bus stop. For a moment he stared back again at the nine floors of the Headquarters of the famous Greater Albion Bay Company.

Like his life the building was now cloaked in silence and darkness.

WEDNESDAY DAY 9

The next morning Arnie arrived on time. Who knows, his times of entry could be recorded on the swipe card so best he never be a minute late.

His head was a whirl. He felt responsible for taking care of things and yet, what a stupid thing to feel when there was nobody to keep the building nice for. But Jim had also said don't give them any pretexts to come back at you later. All night he had pictured how any mistake against him could muddy the waters in some way if they wanted an excuse not to pay him, or to claw money back from him. From what he had seen he wouldn't put that past them, and it's not as if he knew how to represent himself.

He picked up the fallen 'S' from the forecourt and tucked it under his arm, he would put that somewhere safe for now. At the front doors, he got out Jim's huge bunch of keys. After several attempts he found the key to open the revolving doors and then scanned himself through the turnstiles. Immediately the burglar alarm started its slow one minute warning... beep... beep... beep... In no time it would alert the whole neighbourhood and the police.

He bolted across the huge lobby, his footsteps echoing in the empty foyer, his ears pulsing with the relentless warning beeps. At the door to the intake cupboard Arnie fumbled the keys for the right one to open the door, the big 'S' still under his arm. The first two keys would not turn.

The beep was more rapid and louder now. He quickly tried other keys. No luck. Shit! He should have sussed out which key opened this door before he had left yesterday. The beeps came one after the other now, almost on top of each other.

He tried again.

Eventually one turned the lock and Arnie stumbled in, entered the code with fumbling fingers and hit 'Enter'. An error message came up, the deafening beeps now more like a constant siren. He opened his arm to drop the 'S' from under his armpit and typed the password in a second time. He had probably mis-typed it again, but there could only be seconds left so he hit 'Enter' again.

The beeping stopped.

Phew. How many seconds to spare? He didn't want to know.

But for the future he would certainly label which one of these keys opened that bloody door to the intake cupboard, that had cost him 30 seconds at least.

He headed upstairs to Floor 8 and stopped. He glanced at the sign on the door *'Building Services, Manager Mr. J. Slade'*. He could still hear Jim bowling out and saying "...*it's never James. I hate James. It's Jim. Got that, good.*"... "*So work hard, be fair, and you'll love it here...*"

Later when cleaning the trophy cabinet Arnie stopped to look at the bowling cup. The champion three years running two decades ago was one Mr Ron Hutton from the Supplies Team. Arnie smiled, pissing bucket assessment indeed! And there was the darts champion of eight years ago Jim Slade. And under that name was the darts champion for the last six years, a Barry Kox, that must be the tall guy with the beanie hat. And there on the bowling trophy was his old neighbour's name Sue Ragan, the champion five years ago. And Alison Conwenna and Bob Coban were doubles champions last year.

They had kept that one quiet!

The phone pinged. He reached for it and hesitated, this could be contract termination, or another attempted dagger from Lucy. Oh well, let's get this over with.

Hey Arnie, it's Maggie. I've heard from Jim what's going on. Must be so crazy for you. I never got to say goodbye. Hang in there and stay strong! I still say Bessie Smith is better tho! Take good care of yourself, Maggie x

He texted a warm thank you reply and popped the phone back into his pocket. That was so nice of her. She was a good sort really, and she didn't have to take the time to send that text. He had misjudged her at first. A lump filled his throat that made him stop and ponder. Odd how the life-long unappreciated become resilient to it all, only then to be poleaxed when the sudden shock of niceness hits them.

He took a deep breath, hopefully life would be kind to all of them, in whatever they did next.

After a few moments he found himself feeling better. And as his spirits lifted he started to make plans. Right he would work hard, let's get stuck into this bloody trophy cabinet, and then he really would draw up that rota to cover the building as best he could.

"C'mon," he said aloud imitating Slade's voice, "no time for shirkers, moaners, and timewasters."

It made him smile.

* * *

Days passed and rolled into weeks.

Each day Arnie tugged his vacuum cleaner across open seas of empty office floor and steered his scrubber across lobby upon lobby, singing to himself to keep his spirits up. Some days he talked to Tyson. He worked his new rota, stopping only for a brief lunch.

And he had discovered a horde of cleaning stuff in the basement left over from Ron's days. Ron had obviously hidden a secret backup supply. Good ol' Ron. That would keep him going for a good while. It was like Robinson Crusoe finding the shipwreck Arnie had chuckled to himself.

Pride and joy started to fill Arnie as he got on top of things. The only place that beat him was Floor 2. He had tried, but the leftover half-built partitions were scattered everywhere and probably unsafe, some looking like they may topple, others were half fitted and hanging at an assortment of angles. It would take a long time to clear up the mess left by those sloppy contractors. He put hazard signs up and then sat down on a crate and laughed for ten minutes at the madness of it all.

Doubt too crept in some days. Had Jim been right about him still being paid? Even if he would get paid, maybe he should stay at home, surely he would still be entitled to his pay if he didn't come in to work? None of this was his fault, he had simply slipped through a net because of some form. How was he supposed to know the Human Resources Department was going to vanish before his eyes the next day? But on the other hand, what would he then say if they refused to pay him. Eventually he came to a compromise, he would give it to the end of June to see if he was still being paid. If he was, he would carry on and take the money. And if he wasn't paid, he would go home that second.

It seemed to make sense.

On 10 a.m. on the fourth Monday of June Arnie stopped work and sat at Jim's desk. He had made this his own workspace now and had made a nameplate for himself out of inverted cardboard. From here each morning he worked out in what order he would do things that day to best meet his rota. And Monday lunchtimes was what he had called his executive review, when he would sit here and revise the rota to ensure he would use his energies to best effect during the coming week. A tingle of pride and confidence flooded through him as he thought about what he had achieved on his own. He had organised, solved problems, and delivered more than ever now. He gazed at some notes he had made for himself ready for today's executive rota review.

But that was if he was still here by lunchtime today. If he hadn't been paid, he was going home right now.

His fingers fumbling a little he got out his phone and opened the app for his bank. He waited for it to load, holding his breath.

Yes! There in bold letters was the GREATER ALBION BAY COMPANY with his month's salary safely deposited in full and dated Monday 26th June.

He sighed with relief, he needed the money and he wanted to work. He still had a job, and he would carry on doing it, at least until the next pay day at end of July. And if he was paid then, why he'd work through August too. And this lunchtime he had some big decisions to make when revising the rota.

That afternoon in the Pioneers Room Arnie was polishing the old photos that he had once heard Maggie admire. He put down his cloth and gazed more closely, he had never really taken the time to look at them properly before.

Staring back at him were black and white shots of dirty faced pioneer sorts, staring in semi rigid pose at some ancient camera in far off lands as they excavated with nothing but pickaxes, shovels, and hands.

He walked slowly along the row of photos, stopping to peer more closely at some of the faces. He crossed the room to the large picture on the opposite wall, it was of a huge old redbrick Victorian building with two turrets. Below, the brass inscription explained that it had been the original Albion HQ. He looked more closely at the turrets, why there were the same two anchor signs with '*Since 1855*' around them. When Albion had moved in some past era they must have taken those original signs with them. That seals it, that 'S' definitely had to go back up. And he was the only one left to do it. A tricky job but he would finish his next round of the rota and get to that by... He would have to set himself a target date to do it by. He chuckled, 'good old fashioned management that is,' Jim would have said.

Arnie picked up his cloth again and thoroughly cleaned every picture frame. Those pioneer guys deserved it. They were the guys that built all this. And if they were looking down at him from heaven, well he was going to make them proud.

Later, up in the boardroom Arnie walked around like a lone mariner who had boarded the Marie Celeste, faces in grand portraits watching his every move. He looked at them one by one, what would these people have made of Albion today? He shook his head, the long table needed polishing.

Karma would repay him favourably for keeping everything so nice.

Surely.

AUGUST

One sunny morning in late August Arnie decided to eat his lunch outside on the lawn. He wandered to the little raised green bank and sat down to unwrap his pre-packed sandwich. He took a bite of his mature cheese and pickle and looked up at the clear blue sky, he would do this more often until the weather turned in a few weeks' time. It was pleasant lunching here, a pity he hadn't thought of it before.

Almost three months had flown by since he had been left as the last one standing. Mind you, nice as it was, he wouldn't stay here too long today, that Chartwell Suite needed some attention and those lovely art deco features deserved to be kept nice. That place hadn't been touched for a while, what with all the other floors to cover. Maybe he should review his rota again, but not until next Monday lunchtime of course.

As he was munching, he pulled out his phone and started scrolling the clickbait. Most of it was boring celebrity gossip that left him cold. Then a thumbnail heading caught his attention.

'Environmental disaster in Alaska.
Fire rages at Albion Bay site!'

He pressed on the image and read as he ate. The report told of a fire at a disused Albion Bay extraction site that had spread and was now threatening a protected area and wildlife. It was blamed on a negligent contractor that Albion had hired to decommission the site. A spokesperson from something or another was saying this firm had not finished the job properly and not followed regulatory procedures. Now this 'cowboy operation' as the operator was described, had gone into liquidation and the directors could not be found. Investigations were, it said, continuing but the Albion Bay company as the site owner was ultimately responsible. The report then went on to show pictures of devastation and dead wildlife. Poor things muttered Arnie to himself, as he read interviews and quotes from environmental campaigners.

Arnie finished the article and took a swig of his water bottle to wash down the last of the food. That had been a lovely sandwich. He gazed back at the building, that fallen letter from the sign *'ince 1855'* just wasn't looking right. He rubbed his chin, he had an idea how he could get up to do it on his own. So much to do but that job really needed to be done.

Right he said, wiping his hands on his torn overalls as he stood up, it was time to get back to work.

* * *

"How the hell did this happen Marcia?"
"Which one?"

"The Alaskan one."

Mrs Milton looked out of the window of her government offices and put her hands on her hips. A few months to go to retirement and she really did not need a complicated enquiry to round off her thirty five years. She sat down and started looking at the report through the glasses perched on the end of her nose.

Marcia, fifteen years her junior began. "We are starting to get an idea. The defunct contractor hired to decommission the site were registered in the Virgin Islands. The trail has gone cold, it could take a while to track these people down, it looks well dodgy."

"Okay, and the site owner?"

"The Greater Albion Bay Company."

"That's surprising. Up until now they've had an award winning environmental record."

"Well nowadays this is the only site they have left, all the others are either sold off or leased out to be operated by somebody else. It's a very odd one. I've interviewed a key person named Greta Rutherford. She was senior there, a leftover from the days the company was owned by the Hudson Brothers, descendants of the founders. It was a family firm up until recently. This Greta Rutherford resigned in protest having dissented many times previously to the direction the new people were taking. The records confirm what she says."

"Go on."

"Well it seems the firm was taken over by a sharp sort called Mr Devoux, aided by two others, a Mr Friedman and a Mr Gary Yates. In some documents he is known as Gates due to his IT background."

"How original."

"Quite. Anyway I did more digging, and it seems that modernisation was the theme. Outsourcing one of the key strategies. Then one day this Mr Devoux wasn't satisfied with the pace of things. So he set up two separate teams to work independently of each other, one was led by Friedman the other by Gates, I mean Yates. Their task was to compete with each other to see which team could fast track the remainder of the outsourcing the most efficiently."

"And..."

"Well it seems that these two teams, meeting separately, each came up with the same idea that was a bit too clever. To win they would not just outsource the remaining departments, they would also secretly make redundant and outsource the duties of the people in the opposing team."

"So the two teams outsourced each other?"

"Exactly. As well as between them outsourcing everything else. Each team thought they would be left as the only rump. As the remaining core business that would be the one hiring and firing all the new contractors."

"So there was nobody left to hire contractors, or lease out anything else?"

"That's right."

"So the firm ceased to exist in practice."

"That's exactly it."

"And Devoux?"

"Somehow by setting up these competing teams he got caught up in this outsourcing too."

"Pardon?"

"It seems he accidentally outsourced himself!"

"So he's gone too?"

"Apparently. When the locusts had finished there was nothing left of him, or the company."

"The company that ate itself."

"It seems so."

Mrs Milton got up and walked about. "Right well we have to hold somebody responsible for this mess. This Greta Rutherford perhaps?"

"She resigned before all this went into action."

"Companies registration? The company secretary?"

"Nobody left. The two competing teams annulled all registrations of the other team, not realising the other team was doing the same to them. They still have the freehold to some sites dotted around the world, but with Albion having no lease managers the companies operating them have full operational control. Seems they are quite happy to go on working with nobody charging them."

"I bet they are." Mrs Milton sat back down. "Look, this is ridiculous. In time we can launch a full investigation into Devoux, Friedman and Yates. This looks like a minefield."

"Could be kinda hard to nail anyone for anything."

"All that will be after my time Marcia. Right, for now let's focus on the fire and the dodgy firm that botched the decommissioning."

"Quite."

"So Marcia, get a list of people who were last on that Albion payroll and haul in the biggest arse they had left. Nail them to the bloody mast. Whatever they call themselves, Managing Director, Chief whatever...? And if they're too slippery get me the name of the next one down to go after. It's how we've worked all through my service, and I'm damn well not changing it now. And use a discreet back channel to let the press know that we are on the case."

"It should be easy enough to check the payrolls."

Marcia tapped on a screen and waited. "Ah, right, it

seems .... Wait! Golly! It seems there is only one person mentioned on the payroll, a Mr Arnold Horatio Smeggins."

"Just one guy! Is this a darned shadow company?"

"That's all the info we have for now."

"You're sure?"

"Just double checking... yep that's right."

"Ok, get after this Arnold Horatio Smeggins. He must know something if he was the last one standing. Let's bust his arse for all this."

Arnie spent the next morning carrying various lengths of struts and rods outside. He carefully sorted them into their different sizes as he laid them out on the grass in rows. This indoor scaffolding was usually assembled into a mini tower to do the lighting for the higher ceilings inside, but it might just about reach that missing letter outside.

Assembling the unit into the little scaffolding tower was tricky on his own, it was at least a two person job. But once he'd got the basic frame in place it became a lot easier. He'd left the huge castors off the base of the kit, no need to wheel it about for this job like you have do to when you change the lights inside.

A little while later he retrieved the "S" from the lobby. He clambered up the little tower, the gentle summer breeze blowing through the tear in his overalls, making some cloth flap about. He stood on the boards on the top of the scaffold and peered at the fittings on the wall. It just needed rehanging with a few screws in some fresh holes, that would do it for the time being. Easy.

"Are you watching me you pioneers up there!" he yelled as he jumped and punched the sky triumphantly.

A cough from below made him look down. Looking up at him curiously were a huge group of men and women in suits.

Shit.

Behind them followed more people who were pointing phones and cameras at him.

"Who's in charge here?" one of the suited women at the front asked.

* * *

That afternoon Arnie went viral, *'the janitor who stayed behind'* ... *'remember the jungle guy who carries on fighting because he doesn't know the war is over'* ... *'the man they forgot to fire!'* ... and so on. The mainstream media soon picked it up with images on the rolling news channels of him trying to repair the external sign.

That afternoon on the bus home, with a cap pulled down over his forehead and wearing sunglasses, he had watched himself on his phone news stream as the story unfolded. Thankfully he had not been recognised on the bus. Once he got home the radio phone-ins had been about him; ... *tell us when loyalty paid for you ... how to keep going when the world around you quits ... is he nuts or gutsy, tell us your views?....all on the late show tonight.*

Now at just gone eight that evening Arnie lay on his settee with curtains drawn. He had switched off the TV and radio and dimmed the lights. He had had enough. Outside he could hear the rumpus of the media desperate for any morsel they could get, and the occasional banging at the door, or the ringing of the doorbell. And the shouting. The nonstop shouting from the press.

Bang, bang! There it was again.

He heard the letterbox open again. "We just want a few words Arnie, your side of the story. Don't let them spin it against you, put your side out there, just..."

Ring, ring...

Bang, bang...

"Arnie, just a few words..."

He went to the kitchen, poured himself a cool beer, and returned in the dark to his settee, ensuring he made no noise to stir the pack outside again. He sipped his beer, his work at Albion was clearly finished. Now he would have to wait for whatever pay he was owed for August.

The phone pinged, damn had they got hold of his phone number. Hesitantly he looked.

It was from Lucy.

So proud of you Arnie! Malcolm and I have split. He just wasn't you. Always knew you had it in you. Feeling kinda lonely but I suppose I'll survive. Missing you... Lucy xxx

Arnie started to text back, but then paused. After a moment he hit delete, and then removed all Lucy's contact details from his phone for good.

He sprawled out on the settee and covered his head with a towel.

* * *

"A janitor!"

"Yes Mrs Milton."

"Smeggins is a janitor and he's the only employee left!"

"Seems so."

"So what the hell is the Greater Albion Bay Company now, engineering gone, mining gone, CEO gone, staff gone?"

"The once mighty and glorious Greater Albion Bay Company is now just a name and a janitor."

"Absurd."

"I know."

"So what's he been doing?"

"For three months he's been working the entire HQ building on his own."

"What!"

"Apparently he was up some scaffolding trying to fix something when they found him."

"Bloody ridiculous." Mrs Milton got up and walked to her window. "Well the biggest fish in the organisation must answer, that's the law. In this miserable excuse for a company he is the biggest fish. Hell, he's the only fish. I know the rules and precedents didn't exactly envisage this, but let's just fulfil our role and be done with it. Process the case and let the tribunal decide what it wants to do with this. After all Marcia, who are we to judge?"

* * *

A few weeks later Arnie walked into the packed tribunal room. A hum of chatter filled the air as Arnie sat down. He took the sight in, up above the press gallery was bursting, and the room seemed full of official looking people typing like mad.

Arnie took the oath and waited.

Three officials sat at the bench at the front. The central one addressed him, "Mr Smeggins, before we begin, do you have any opening statement that can help throw light on events?"

"It began with my mop."

"Your what?"

"My mop."

"Your mop?"

"Yes, well the empty cupboards really, but I was already planning to go back down about my mop anyway."

"Would you please clarify..."

"Well you see I was sort of promised another one on the first day and then after the cupboards weren't stocked everything seemed to go astray. From my viewpoint it all led from that really."

"You wanted a mop?"

"Well a second one in truth. Builder's dust everywhere, it ruins the head. Not just a mop, all my supplies. That's how my overalls got torn."

"Your overalls?"

"Yes. On the toilet window. When the burglar alarms went off. After I went out to get gear and couldn't get back in."

"Mr Smeggins..."

"I can't do my job without the equipment and that's all I wanted to do."

"What is?"

"My duty. I just wanted to do my duty for Albion."

"Thank you, Mr Smeggins," intervened the chair. He turned to some suits at the front, "May I have a word?"

A few individuals approached the front as Arnie strained to hear. There was barely audible muttering from the sudden huddle at the front.

"In terms of gathering the facts, if there are no objections I am not sure there is anything material to be gained here. We have clarification that Mr Smeggins had no authority in the company for which he can be held liable when the operational decisions were taken. In terms of his unusual status at the end, do either of you have any objections that we accept the evidence from a Mr James Slade and a Mr Sandeep Singh as to how Mr Smeggins came to be the last named employee of this company?"

"*None.*"

"*So on that singular point all parties are agreed?*"

"*Aye.*"

"*Well in that case, get him out of here!*"

And a hundred cameras flashed

EPILOGUE

Early one morning during that following autumn, Arnie was woken by the chime of his doorbell. He checked the time on his phone, blearily put on a dressing gown, and wandered yawning and stretching to get his front door. He opened it and blinked twice in the bright, crisp autumnal sunlight.

"Maggie!"

"Morning Arnie!"

"What the...?"

"Get dressed and come with me."

"What at this time?"

"That's right."

"Why, is Bessie Smith alive somewhere?"

"Ha-ha, if she was I wouldn't be talking to you. Now go get dressed, I'll wait."

"Where are we going?"

"You'll see."

"How did you know I wouldn't already be out at work somewhere?"

"I didn't until now."

"Oh right. Er you better come in," he said rubbing his eye. "It's a bit of a mess I'm afraid."

"It's ok Arnie, it's a nice day I'll wait outside here."

A little while later Arnie emerged into the fresh air, pulling his puffer jacket on as he locked the door of his ground floor apartment. Maggie was standing by a car across the street and waved to attract him.

"So what's all this about?" Arnie asked as he got in.

"You'll see," Maggie started the car up and pulled away.

"It had better be good," Arnie yawned as he gazed in the vanity mirror and saw his unshaven face, his thinning hair still stubbornly sticking up all over the place.

"So have you been keeping well Arnie?"

"Kinda, you Maggie?"

"Never better Arnie."

"That's good."

Maggie paused. "Arnie you seem different."

"How so?"

"I don't know just different."

"For the better?"

"Are you fishing for compliments Arnie?" Maggie gave a slight sideways glance-come-half-smile from the driving seat.

"Maybe," Arnie joked.

They both chuckled.

Maggie turned on the music player. Scrapper Blackwell's *Nobody Knows You* filled the car with old blues.

"Good taste," Arnie teased.

Ten minutes later the car pulled up and they both got out.

"Come on," said Maggie, "follow me, it's just around the corner."

Arnie yawned again and hauled himself out of the car.

They walked through a few side streets and a moment later emerged into a large, paved square. On the other side of the square was a large redbrick Victorian building with a turret on either side. Arnie gazed at it as they approached, he knew this place from somewhere. Then two huge anchor emblems on either turret came into view, with the words '*Since 1855*' emblazoned below them.

Arnie looked at Maggie with a sort of '*this can't be what I think it might be*' sort of look.

Maggie replied with a half-smile and a faint nod.

"You're not serious...?"

Maggie just nodded again as they approached the entrance.

"Good to see you Arnie," said Sue following up behind.

Arnie turned, "Sue!!"

"All back up and running," explained Maggie. "Only there's some legal problem using the other building. So it's back to the original HQ here."

"But how?"

"No point a sound business not making money," said Sue stopping with them. "Well that's what young Mrs Hudson and her family think anyway. Especially with all that staff expertise and organisational memory on hand."

"What does organisational memory mean?" asked Arnie.

"Don't worry," said Sue. "Google that later, but it's gold dust."

At that Arnie had to step out of the way as a figure came barging through like a rugby player breaking the line...

"Morning Arnie," Ali said charging by, "great to see you!"

"Morning Ali," Arnie stammered pivoting around 180 degrees, "good to see you too."

"Hi Arnie..." said another voice passing on the other side of him.

Arnie pivoted back 180 degrees the other way, "Hey Bob!"

"Hey Arnie, fancy that risotto?" said a voice back the other side of Arnie.

"Hey Salvo, good to see you," said Arnie spinning back again as traders and operations managers started filing by, bidding him good morning.

Arnie gazed at Maggie and Sue.

"The old gang are back," explained Maggie. "They can't buy all the sold excavation sites back of course, so damage was done, but they're renting sites around the world, managing sites for other companies, and starting to acquire some new ones."

"Indeed," said Sue. "By the way Maggie, did you hear that the Hudson family have appointed Greta as the new Chief Exec. And I'll be helping her upstairs now."

"Congratulations Sue," Maggie beamed, "you deserve it. Any latest on Devoux, Friedman, Yates?"

"Nothing yet on Devoux, but it could go on forever. Greta told me she and the Hudson family want backroom staff to serve frontline work, not the other way around."

"How refreshing these days."

"So no place for Friedman," continued Sue. "I guess he'll go back to being a head accountant somewhere. Or into politics or local government where his ideas will sound persuasive, so long as nobody asks what happens when the rubber hits the road."

Maggie smiled. "I think it was more groupthink that all these so-called modernising things are automatically the way to go on everything, regardless of whether they fit or are needed. Or if they work. More incompetence than nastiness."

"Well not anymore. Greta says we'll modernise as we have always done, as and when it suits us best. Not just for the sake of it. And we'll outsource, but only when it's the best option, and even then only after weighing up all the hidden costs and losses it brings. And it won't be the easy way out for executives who can't manage teams anymore. Her words."

"And Yates?" asked Maggie.

"Greta says IT will support frontline work, not distract it. The very idea was too much for poor Gary Yates. He tried but he just couldn't get his head around the idea. He took unwell. I hear he has gone to a retreat in North Wales and is taking a long sabbatical to recover from the thought."

"Oh dear, perhaps he'll get over it in a year or two," said Maggie.

"Ah bless him," laughed Sue. "Fleetwood will head our small new IT team. Greta's given them a stern brief not to try to justify their existence with any..."

Arnie felt a tap on his shoulder.

"Morning Arnie," said a familiar voice.

"Hey Sandeep!"

"Welcome back to the team Arnie."

"What?"

"I said welcome back to..."

"Yes I heard what you said....you mean...?"

Sue and Maggie stood smiling.

"Why sure Arnie," Sandeep beamed. "You're the company celebrity. It was your perseverance that inspired young Mrs Hudson to step back in, and your incredible loyalty requires loyalty back. So of course you have your job back if you want it, and with higher pay, the global exposure you brought us is a winner in an otherwise embarrassingly sad Albion story. And Greta wants to see you later with a golden hello as well."

"Why well of course yes."

"Good, come to HR to sign the forms. And don't forget this time!"

"I won't."

"Hey Arnie," said Bob popping his head out of the door, "bloody well hurry up will ya, I need a hand in here."

"This is wonderful," said Arnie as he waved a hello at Roger just inside the entrance, "and are you back too Maggie?"

"No Arnie, I'm the only one missing. Hasna is the head of Marketing now. I only decided yesterday, I'd love to return with Greta in charge, but I declined the offer. I'm taking some time out to finish writing my book on the old blues. It's a life decision. I have my own take on it and if I don't finish it now, well it will never happen."

"Good for you, hey and don't forget to give old Scrapper a good mention."

"Ha-ha, thanks to you I will."

"Let's see what life is like after Maggie," smiled Sue disappearing inside with Sandeep.

"And Arnie, you know what this also means?" said Maggie when they were alone.

"No."

"It means you're no longer a colleague in a company I work for. So I wondered if you'd like a drink with me later. I know a great little blues bar and it'd be nice if I had somebody to go with, someone who knows the old blues too. It's Delta blues tonight if you fancy it. I'll get there about 8.30, I'll text you the address?"

"Er...why sure Maggie, yeah love to. See you tonight."

At that Slade bowled out of the entrance. "Come on Arnie, get yourself down to Ron to get your gear. Don't push your luck and ask for two mops though. No time for shirkers, moaners, or timewasters, we all work together here. Got that, good."

Maggie nodded towards Slade, "You'd better go in."

Arnie smiled as he turned, "Later it is then."

"Got that, good," she replied smiling back.

-END-

I am grateful to all who offered their generous support in the production of this work, but particular thanks to Gideon, Paula, and Steve for their fine reviews and unwavering encouragement, and to Kay for her ever so patient proofreading.